Leixlip Castle

and other tales

by

Charles Robert Maturin

Honoré de Balzac

Guy de Maupassant

Anonymous

Contents

Leixlip Castle

by Charles Robert Maturin

THE incidents of the following tale are not merely *founded on* fact, they are facts themselves, which occurred at no very distant period in my own family. The marriage of the parties, their sudden and mysterious separation, and their total alienation from each other until the last period of their mortal existence, are all *facts*. I cannot vouch for the truth of the supernatural solution given to all these mysteries; but I must still consider the story as a fine specimen of Gothic horrors, and can never forget the impression it made on me when I heard it related for the first time among many other thrilling traditions of the same description.

C.R.M.

The tranquillity of the Catholics of Ireland during the disturbed periods of 1715 and 1745, was most commendable, and somewhat extraordinary; to enter into an analysis of their probable motives, is not at all the object of the writer of this tale, as it is pleasanter to state the fact of their honour, than at this distance of time to assign dubious and unsatisfactory reasons for it. Many of them, however, showed a kind of secret disgust at the existing state of affairs, by quitting their family residences and wandering about like persons who were uncertain of their homes, or possibly expecting better from some near and fortunate contingency.

Among the rest was a Jacobite Baronet, who, sick of his uncongenial situation in a Whig neighbourhood, in the north — where he heard of nothing but the heroic defence of Londonderry; the barbarities of the French generals; and the resistless exhortations of the godly Mr Walker, a Presbyterian clergyman, to whom the citizens gave the title of 'Evangelist'; — quitted his paternal residence, and about the year 1720 hired the Castle of Leixlip for three years (it was then the property of the Connollys, who let it to triennial tenants); and removed thither with his family, which consisted of three daughters — their mother having long been dead.

The Castle of Leixlip, at that period, possessed a character of romantic beauty and feudal grandeur, such as few buildings in Ireland can claim, and which is now, alas, totally effaced by the destruction of its noble woods; on the destroyers of which the writer would wish 'a minstrel's malison were said'. — Leixlip, though about seven miles from Dublin, has all the sequestered and picturesque character that imagination could ascribe to a landscape a hundred miles from, not only the metropolis but an inhabited town. After driving a dull mile (an Irish mile) in passing from Lucan to Leixlip, the road — hedged up on one side of the high wall that bounds the demesne of the Veseys, and on the other by low enclosures, over whose rugged tops you have no view at all — at once opens on Leixlip Bridge, at almost a right angle, and displays a luxury of landscape on which the eye that has seen it even in childhood dwells with delighted recollection. — Leixlip Bridge, a rude but solid structure, projects from a high bank of the Liffey, and slopes rapidly to the opposite side, which there lies remarkably low. To the right the plantations of the Vesey's demesne — no longer obscured by walls — almost mingle their dark woods in its stream, with the opposite ones of Marshfield and St Catherine's. The river is scarcely visible, overshadowed as it is by the deep, rich and bending foliage of the trees. To the left it bursts out in all the brilliancy of light, washes the garden steps of the houses of Leixlip, wanders round the low walls of its churchyard, plays, with the pleasure-boat moored under the arches on which the summer-house of the Castle is raised, and then loses itself among the rich woods that once skirted those grounds to its very brink. The contrast on the other side, with the luxuriant walks, scattered shrubberies, temples seated on pinnacles, and thickets that conceal from you the sight of the river until you are on its banks, that mark the character of the grounds which are now the property of Colonel Marly, is peculiarly striking.

Visible above the highest roofs of the town, though a quarter of a mile distant from them, are the ruins of Confy Castle, a right good old predatory tower of the stirring times when blood was shed like water; and as you pass the bridge you catch a glimpse of the waterfall (or salmon-leap, as it is called) on whose noon-day lustre, or moon-light beauty, probably the rough livers of that age when Confy Castle was 'a tower of strength', never glanced an eye or cast a thought, as they clattered in their harness over Leixlip Bridge, or waded through the stream before that convenience was in existence.

Whether the solitude in which he lived contributed to tranquillize Sir Redmond Blaney's feelings, or whether they had begun to rust from want of collision with those of others, it is impossible to say, but certain it is, that the good Baronet began gradually to lose his tenacity in political matters; and except when a Jacobite friend came to dine with him, and drink with many a significant 'nod and beck and smile', the King over the water — or the parish-priest (good man) spoke of the hopes of better times, and the final success of the *right* cause, and the old religion —or a Jacobite servant was heard in the solitude of the large mansion whistling 'Charlie is my darling', to which Sir Redmond involuntarily responded in a deep bass voice, somewhat the worse for wear, and marked with more emphasis than good discretion — except, as I have said, on such occasions, the Baronet's politics, like his life, seemed passing away without notice or effort. Domestic calamities, too, pressed sorely on the old gentleman: of his three daughters the youngest, Jane, had disappeared in so

3

extraordinary a manner in her childhood, that though it is but a wild, remote family tradition, I cannot help relating it:

The girl was of uncommon beauty and intelligence, and was suffered to wander about the neighbourhood of the castle with the daughter of a servant, who was also called Jane, as a *nom de caresse*. One evening Jane Blaney and her young companion went far and deep into the woods; their absence created no uneasiness at the time, as these excursions were by no means unusual, till her playfellow returned home alone and weeping, at a very late hour. Her account was, that, in passing through a lane at some distance from the castle, an old woman, in the *Fingallian* dress, (a red petticoat and a long green jacket), suddenly started out of a thicket, and took Jane Blaney by the arm: she had in her hand two rushes, one of which she threw over her shoulder, and giving the other to the child, motioned to her to do the same. Her young companion, terrified at what she saw, was running away, when Jane Blaney called after her — 'Good-bye, good-bye, it is a long time before you will see me again.' The girl said they then disappeared, and she found her way home as she could. An indefatigable search was immediately commenced — woods were traversed, thickets were explored, ponds were drained — all in vain. The pursuit and the hope were at length given up. Ten years afterwards, the housekeeper of Sir Redmond, having remembered that she left the key of a closet where sweetmeats were kept, on the kitchen table, returned to fetch it. As she approached the door, she heard a childish voice murmuring — 'Cold — cold — cold how long it is since I have felt a fire!' — She advanced, and saw, to her amazement, Jane Blaney, shrunk to half her usual size, and covered with rags, crouching over the embers of the fire. The housekeeper flew in terror from the spot, and roused the servants, but the vision had fled. The child was reported to have been seen several times afterwards, as diminutive in form, as though she had not grown an inch since she was ten years of age, and always crouching over a fire, whether in the turret-room or kitchen, complaining of cold and hunger, and apparently covered with rags. Her existence is still said to be

4

protracted under these dismal circumstances, so unlike those of Lucy Gray in Wordsworth's beautiful ballad:

Yet some will say, that to this day
She is a living child -
That they have met sweet Lucy Gray
Upon the lonely wild;
O'er rough and smooth she trips along,
And never looks behind;
And hums a solitary song
That whistles in the wind.

The fate of the eldest daughter was more melancholy, though less extraordinary; she was addressed by a gentleman of competent fortune and unexceptionable character: he was a Catholic, moreover; and Sir Redmond Blaney signed the marriage articles, in full satisfaction of the security of his daughter's soul, as well as of her jointure. The marriage was celebrated at the Castle of Leixlip; and, after the bride and bridegroom had retired, the guests still remained drinking to their future happiness, when suddenly, to the great alarm of Sir Redmond and his friends, loud and piercing cries were heard to issue from the part of the castle in which the bridal chamber was situated.

Some of the more courageous hurried up stairs; it was too late — the wretched bridegroom had burst, on that fatal night, into a sudden and most horrible paroxysm of insanity. The mangled form of the unfortunate and expiring lady bore attestation to the mortal virulence with which the disease had operated on the wretched husband, who died a victim to it himself after the involuntary murder of his bride. The bodies were interred, as soon as decency would permit, and the story hushed up.

Sir Redmond's hopes of Jane's recovery were diminishing every day, though he still continued to listen to every wild tale told by the domestics; and all his care was supposed to be now directed towards his only surviving daughter. Anne, living in solitude, and partaking only of the very limited education of Irish females of that period, was left very much to the servants, among whom she increased her taste for superstitious and supernatural horrors, to a degree that had a most disastrous effect on her future life.

Among the numerous menials of the Castle, there was one withered crone, who had been nurse to the late Lady Blaney's mother, and whose memory was a complete *Thesaurus terrorum*. The mysterious fate of Jane first encouraged her sister to listen to the wild tales of this hag, who avouched, that at one time she saw the fugitive standing before the portrait of her late mother in one of the apartments of the Castle, and muttering to herself — 'Woe's me, woe's me! how little my mother thought her wee Jane would ever come to be what she is!' But as Anne grew older she began more 'seriously to incline' to the hag's promises that she could show her her future bridegroom, on the performance of certain ceremonies, which she at first revolted from as horrible and impious; but, finally. at the repeated instigation of the old woman, consented to act a part in. The period fixed upon for the performance of these unhallowed rites, was now approaching — it was near the 31st of October — the eventful night, when such ceremonies were, and still are supposed, in the North of Ireland, to be most potent in their effects. All day long the Crone took care to lower the mind of the young lady to the proper key of submissive and trembling credulity, by every horrible story she could relate; and she told them with frightful and supernatural energy. This woman was called *Collogue* by the family, a name equivalent to Gossip in England, or Cummer in Scotland (though her real name was Bridget Dease); and she verified the name, by the exercise of an unwearied loquacity, an indefatigable memory, and a rage for communicating and inflicting terror, that spared no victim in the household, from the groom, whom she sent shivering to his rug, to the Lady of the Castle, over whom she felt she held unbounded sway.

The 31st of October arrived — the Castle was perfectly quiet before eleven o'clock; half an hour afterwards, the Collogue and Anne Blaney were seen gliding along a passage

6

that led to what is called King John's Tower, where it is said that monarch received the homage of the Irish princes as Lord of Ireland and which was, at all events, the most ancient part of the structure.

The Collogue opened a small door with a key which she had secreted, about her, and urged the young lady to hurry on. Anne advanced to the postern, and stood there irresolute and trembling like a timid swimmer on the bank of an unknown stream. It was a dark autumnal evening; a heavy wind sighed among the woods of the Castle, and bowed the branches of the lower trees almost to the waves of the Liffey, which, swelled by recent rains, struggled and roared amid the stones that obstructed its channel. The steep descent from the Castle lay before her, with its dark avenue of elms; a few lights still burned in the little village of Leixlip — but from the lateness of the hour it was probable they would soon be extinguished.

The lady lingered — 'And must I go alone?' said she, foreseeing that the terrors of her fearful journey could be aggravated by her more fearful purpose.

'Ye must, or all will be spoiled,' said the hag, shading the miserable light, that did not extend its influence above six inches on the path of the victim. 'Ye must go alone — and I will watch for you here, dear, till you come back, and then see what will come to you at twelve o'clock.'

The unfortunate girl paused. 'Oh! Collogue, Collogue, if you would but come with me. Oh! Collogue, come with me, if it be but to the bottom of the castle hill.'

'If I went with you, dear, we should never reach the top of it alive again, for there are them near that would tear us both in pieces.'

'Oh! Collogue, Collogue — let me turn back then, and go to my own room — I have advanced too far, and I have done too much.'

'And that's what you have, dear, and so you must go further, and do more still, unless, when you return to your own room, you would see the likeness of *some one* instead of a handsome young bridegroom.'

The young lady looked about her for a moment, terror and wild hope trembling at her heart — then, with a sudden impulse of supernatural courage, she darted like a bird from the terrace of the Castle, the fluttering of her white garments was seen for a few moments, and then the hag who had been shading the flickering light with her hand, bolted the postern, and, placing the candle before a glazed loophole, sat down on a stone seat in the recess of the tower, to watch the event of the spell. It was an hour before the young lady returned; when her face was as pale, and her eyes as fixed, as those of a dead body, but she held in her grasp *a dripping garment,* a proof that her errand had been performed. She flung it into her companion's hands, and then stood, panting and gazing wildly about her as if she knew not where she was. The hag herself grew terrified at the insane and breathless state of her victim, and hurried her to her chamber; but here the preparations for the terrible ceremonies of the night were the first objects that struck her, and, shivering at the sight, she covered her eyes with her hands, and stood immovably fixed in the middle of the room.

It needed all the hag's persuasions (aided even by mysterious menaces), combined with the returning faculties and reviving curiosity of the poor girl, to prevail on her to go through the remaining business of the night. At length she said, as if in desperation, 'I *will* go through with it: but be in the next room; and if what I dread should happen, I will ring my father's little silver bell which I have secured for the night — and as you have a soul to be saved, Collogue, come to me at its first sound.'

The hag promised, gave her last instructions with eager and jealous minuteness, and then retired to her own room, which was adjacent to that of the young lady. Her candle had burned out, but she stirred up the embers of her turf fire, and sat, nodding over them, and smoothing the pallet from time to time, but resolved not to lie down while there was a chance of a sound from the lady's room, for which she herself, withered as her feelings were, waited with a mingled feeling of anxiety and terror.

It was now long past midnight, and all was silent as the grave throughout the Castle. The hag dozed over the embers till her head touched her knees, then started up as the sound of the bell seemed to tinkle in her ears, then dozed again, and again started as the bell appeared to tinkle more distinctly — suddenly she was roused, not by the bell, but by the most piercing and horrible cries from the neighbouring chamber. The Collogue, aghast for the first time, at the possible consequences of the mischief she might have occasioned, hastened to the room. Anne was in convulsions, and the hag was compelled reluctantly to call up the housekeeper (removing meanwhile the implements of the ceremony), and assist in applying all the specifics known at that day, burnt feathers, etc., to restore her. When they had at length succeeded, the housekeeper was dismissed, the door was bolted, and the Collogue was left alone with Anne; the subject of their conference might have been guessed at, but was not known until many years afterwards; but Anne that night held in her hand, in the shape of a weapon with the use of which neither of them was acquainted, an evidence that her chamber had been visited by a being of no earthly form.

This evidence the hag importuned her to destroy, or to remove: but she persisted with fatal tenacity in keeping it. She locked it up, however, immediately, and seemed to think she had acquired a right, since she had grappled so fearfully with the mysteries of futurity, to know all the secrets of which that weapon might yet lead to the disclosure. But from that night it was observed that her character, her manner, and even her countenance, became altered. She grew stern and solitary, shrunk at the sight of her former associates, and imperatively forbade the slightest allusion to the circumstances which had occasioned this mysterious change.

It was a few days subsequent to this event that Anne, who after dinner had left the Chaplain reading the life of St Francis Xavier to Sir Redmond, and retired to her own room to work, and, perhaps, to muse, was surprised to hear the bell at the outer gate ring loudly and repeatedly — a sound she had never heard since her first residence in the Castle; for the few guests who resorted there came, and departed as noiselessly as humble visitors at the house of a great man generally do. Straightway there rode up the avenue of elms, which we have already mentioned, a stately gentleman, followed by four servants, all mounted, the two former having pistols in their holsters, and the two latter carrying saddle-bags before them: though it was the first week in November, the dinner hour being one o'clock, Anne had light enough to notice all these circumstances. The arrival of the stranger seemed to cause much, though not unwelcome tumult in the Castle; orders were loudly and hastily given for the accommodation of the servants and horses — steps were heard traversing the numerous passages for a full hour — then all was still; and it was said that Sir Redmond had locked with his own hand the door of the room where he and the stranger sat, and desired that no one should dare to approach it. About two hours afterwards, a female servant came with orders from her master, to have a plentiful supper ready by eight o'clock, at which he desired the presence of his daughter. The family establishment was on a handsome scale for an Irish house, and Anne had only to descend to the kitchen to order the roasted chickens to be well strewed with brown sugar according to the unrefined fashion of the day, to inspect the mixing of the bowl of sago with its allowance of a bottle of port wine and a large handful of the richest spices, and to order particularly that the pease pudding should have a huge lump of cold salt butter stuck in its centre; and then, her household cares being over, to retire to her room and array herself in a robe of white damask for the occasion. At eight o'clock she was summoned to the supper-room. She came in, according to the fashion of the times, with the first dish; but as she passed through the ante-room, where the servants were holding lights and bearing the dishes, her sleeve was twitched, and the ghastly face of the Collogue pushed close to hers; while she muttered 'Did not I say *he would come for* you, dear?' Anne's blood ran cold, but she advanced, saluted her father and the stranger with two low and distinct reverences, and then took her place at the table. Her feelings of awe and perhaps terror at the whisper of her associate, were not diminished by the appearance of the stranger; there was a singular and mute solemnity in his manner during the meal. He ate nothing. Sir Redmond appeared constrained, gloomy and thoughtful. At length, starting, he said (without naming the stranger's name), 'You will drink my daughter's health?' The stranger intimated his willingness to have that honour, but absently filled his glass with water; Anne put a few drops of wine into hers, and bowed towards him. At that moment, for the first time since they had met, she beheld his face — it was pale as that of a corpse. The deadly whiteness of his cheeks and lips, the hollow and distant sound of his voice, and the strange lustre of his large dark moveless eyes, strongly fixed on her, made her pause and even tremble as she raised the glass to her lips; she set it down, and then with another silent reverence retired to her chamber.

There she found Bridget Dease, busy in collecting the turf that burned on the hearth, for there was no grate in the apartment. 'Why are you here?' she said, impatiently.

The hag turned on her, with a ghastly grin of congratulation, 'Did not I tell you that *he* would come for you?'

'I believe he has,' said the unfortunate girl, sinking into the huge wicker chair by her bedside; 'for never did I see mortal with such a look.'

'But is not he a fine stately gentleman?' pursued the hag.

'He looks as if he were not of this world,' said Anne.

'Of this world, or of the next,' said the hag, raising her bony fore-finger, 'mark my words —so sure as the — (here she repeated some of the horrible formularies of the 31st of October) — so sure he will be your bridegroom.'

'Then I shall be the bride of a corpse,' said Anne; 'for he I saw tonight is no living man.'

11

A fortnight elapsed, and whether Anne became reconciled to the features she had thought so ghastly, by the discovery that they were the handsomest she had ever beheld — and that the voice, whose sound at first was so strange and unearthly, was subdued into a tone of plaintive softness when addressing her or whether it is impossible for two young persons with unoccupied hearts to meet in the country, and meet often, to gaze silently on the same stream, wander under the same trees, and listen together to the wind that waves the branches, without experiencing an assimilation of feeling rapidly succeeding an assimilation of taste; — or whether it was from all these causes combined, but in less than a month Anne heard the declaration of the stranger's passion with many a blush, though without a sigh. He now avowed his name and rank. He stated himself to be a Scottish Baronet, of the name of Sir Richard Maxwell; family misfortunes had driven him from his country, and forever precluded the possibility of his return: he had transferred his property to Ireland, and purposed to fix his residence there for life. Such was his statement. The courtship of those days was brief and simple. Anne became the wife of Sir Richard, and, I believe, they resided with her father till his death, when they removed to their estate in the North. There they remained for several years, in tranquillity and happiness, and had a numerous family. Sir Richard's conduct was marked by but two peculiarities: he not only shunned the intercourse, but the sight of any of his countrymen, and, if he happened to hear that a Scotsman had arrived in the neighbouring town, he shut himself up till assured of the stranger's departure. The other was his custom of retiring to his own chamber, and remaining invisible to his family on the anniversary of the 31st of October. The lady, who had her own associations connected with that period, only questioned him once on the subject of this seclusion, and was then solemnly and even sternly enjoined never to repeat her inquiry. Matters stood thus, somewhat mysteriously, but not unhappily, when on a sudden, without any cause assigned or assignable, Sir Richard and Lady Maxwell parted, and never more met in this world, nor was she ever permitted to see one of her children to her dying hour. He continued to live at the family mansion and she fixed her residence with a distant relative in a remote part of the country. So total was the disunion, that the name of either was never heard to pass the other's lips, from the moment of separation until that of dissolution.

Lady Maxwell survived Sir Richard forty years, living to the great age of ninety-six; and, according to a promise, previously given, disclosed to a descendent with whom she had lived, the following extraordinary circumstances.

She said that on the night of the 31st of October, about seventy-five years before, at the instigation of her ill-advising attendant, she had washed one of her garments in a place where four streams met, and performed other unhallowed ceremonies under the direction of the Collogue, in the expectation that her future husband would appear to her in her chamber at twelve o'clock that night. The critical moment arrived, but with it no lover-like form. A vision of indescribable horror approached her bed, and flinging at her an iron weapon of a shape and construction unknown to her, bade her 'recognize her future husband *by that.*' The terrors of this visit soon deprived her of her senses; but on her recovery, she persisted, as has been said, in keeping the fearful pledge of the reality of the vision, which, on examination, appeared to be incrusted with blood. It remained concealed in the inmost drawer of her cabinet till the morning of the separation. On that morning, Sir Richard Maxwell rose before daylight to join a hunting party — he wanted a knife for some accidental purpose, and, missing his own, called to Lady Maxwell, who was still in bed, to lend him one. The lady, who was half asleep, answered, that in such a drawer of her cabinet he would find one. He went, however, to another, and the next moment she was fully awakened by seeing her husband present the terrible weapon to her throat, and threaten her with instant death unless she disclosed how she came by it. She supplicated for life, and then, in an agony of horror and contrition, told the tale of that eventful night. He gazed at her for a moment with a countenance which rage, hatred, and despair converted, as she avowed, into a living likeness of the demon-visage she had once beheld (so singularly was the fated resemblance fulfilled), and then exclaiming, 'You won me by the devil's aid, but you shall not keep me long,' left her — to meet no more in this world. Her husband's secret was not unknown to the lady, though the means by which she became possessed of it were wholly unwarrantable. Her curiosity had been strongly excited by her husband's aversion to his countrymen, and it was so — stimulated by the arrival of a Scottish gentleman in the neighbourhood some time before, who professed himself formerly acquainted with Sir Richard, and spoke mysteriously of the causes that drove him from his country — that she contrived to procure an interview with him under a feigned name, and obtained from him the knowledge of circumstances which embittered her after-life to its latest hour. His story was this:

Sir Richard Maxwell was at deadly feud with a younger brother; a family feast was proposed to reconcile them, and as the use of knives and forks was then unknown in the Highlands, the company met armed with their dirks for the purpose of carving. They drank deeply; the feast, instead of harmonizing, began to inflame their spirits; the topics of old strife were renewed; hands, that at first touched their weapons in defiance, drew them at last in fury, and in the fray, Sir Richard mortally wounded his brother. His life was with difficulty saved from the vengeance of the clan, and he was hurried towards the seacoast, near which the house stood, and concealed there till a vessel could be procured to convey him to Ireland. He embarked *on the night of the 31st of October,* and while he was traversing the deck in unutterable agony of spirit, his hand accidentally touched the dirk which he had unconsciously worn ever since the fatal night. He drew it, and, praying 'that the guilt of his brother's blood might be as far from his soul, as he could fling that weapon from his body,' sent it with all his strength into the air. This instrument he found secreted in the lady's cabinet, and whether he really believed her to have become possessed of it by supernatural means, or whether he feared his wife was a secret witness of his crime, has not been ascertained, but the result was what I have stated.

The separation took place on the discovery: — for the rest,

> I know not how the truth may be,
> I tell the Tale as 'twas told to me.

Melmoth the Wanderer
(abridged)
by *Charles Robert Maturin*

John Melmoth, student at Trinity College, Dublin, having journeyed to County Wicklow for attendance at the deathbed of his miserly uncle, finds the old man, even in his last moments, tortured by avarice, and by suspicion of all around him. He whispers to John:

"I want a glass of wine, it would keep me alive for some hours, but there is not one I can trust to get it for me,—they'd steal a bottle, and ruin me." John was greatly shocked. "Sir, for God's sake, let ME get a glass of wine for you." "Do you know where?" said the old man, with an expression in his face John could not understand. "No, Sir; you know I have been rather a stranger here, Sir." "Take this key," said old Melmoth, after a violent spasm; "take this key, there is wine in that closet,—Madeira. I always told them there was nothing there, but they did not believe me, or I should not have been robbed as I have been. At one time I said it was whisky, and then I fared worse than ever, for they drank twice as much of it."

John took the key from his uncle's hand; the dying man pressed it as he did so, and John, interpreting this as a mark of kindness, returned the pressure. He was undeceived by the whisper that followed,—"John, my lad, don't drink any of that wine while you are there." "Good God!" said John, indignantly throwing the key on the bed; then, recollecting that the miserable being before him was no object of resentment, he gave the promise required, and entered the closet, which no foot but that of old Melmoth had entered for nearly sixty years. He had some difficulty in finding out the wine, and indeed stayed long enough to justify his uncle's suspicions,—but his mind was agitated, and his hand unsteady. He could not but remark his uncle's extraordinary look, that had the ghastliness of fear superadded to that of death, as he gave him permission to enter his closet. He could not but see the looks of horror which the women exchanged as he approached it. And, finally, when he was in it, his memory was malicious enough to suggest some faint traces of a story, too horrible for imagination, connected with it. He remembered in one moment most distinctly, that no one but his uncle had ever been known to enter it for many years.

Before he quitted it, he held up the dim light, and looked around him with a mixture of terror and curiosity. There was a great deal of decayed and useless lumber, such as might be supposed to be heaped up to rot in a miser's closet; but John's eyes were in a moment, and as if by magic, riveted on a portrait that hung on the wall, and appeared, even to his untaught eye, far superior to the tribe of family pictures that are left to moulder on the walls of a family mansion. It represented a man of middle age. There was nothing remarkable in the costume, or in the countenance, but THE EYES, John felt, were such as one feels they wish they had never seen, and feels they can never forget. Had he been acquainted with the poetry of Southey, he might have often exclaimed in his after-life,

"Only the eyes had life,
    They gleamed with demon light."—THALABA.

From an impulse equally resistless and painful, he approached the portrait, held the candle toward it, and could distinguish the words on the border of the painting,—Jno. Melmoth, anno 1646. John was neither timid by nature, nor nervous by constitution, nor superstitious from habit, yet he continued to gaze in stupid horror on this singular picture, till, aroused by his uncle's cough, he hurried into his room. The old man swallowed the wine. He appeared a little revived; it was long since he had tasted such a cordial,—his heart appeared to expand to a momentary confidence. "John, what did you see in that room?" "Nothing, Sir." "That's a lie; everyone wants to cheat or to rob me." "Sir, I don't want to do either." "Well, what did you see that you—you took notice of?" "Only a picture, Sir." "A picture, Sir!—the original is still alive." John, though under the impression of his recent feelings, could not but look incredulous. "John," whispered his uncle;— "John, they say I am dying of this and that; and one says it is for want of nourishment, and one says it is for want of medicine,—but, John," and his face looked hideously ghastly, "I am dying of a fright. That man," and he extended his meagre arm toward the closet, as if he was pointing to a living being; "that man, I have good reason to know, is alive still." "How is that possible, Sir?" said John involuntarily, "the date on the picture is 1646." "You have seen it,—you have noticed it," said his uncle. "Well,"—he rocked and nodded on his bolster for a moment, then, grasping John's hand with an unutterable look, he exclaimed, "You will see him again, he is alive." Then, sinking back on his bolster, he fell into a kind of sleep or stupor, his eyes still open, and fixed on John.

The house was now perfectly silent, and John had time and space for reflection. More thoughts came crowding on him than he wished to welcome, but they would not be repulsed. He thought of his uncle's habits and character, turned the matter over and over again in his mind, and he said to himself, "The last man on earth to be superstitious. He never thought of anything but the price of stocks, and the rate of exchange, and my college expenses, that hung heavier at his heart than all; and such a man to die of a fright,—a ridiculous fright, that a man living 150 years ago is alive still, and yet—he is dying." John paused, for facts will confute the most stubborn logician. "With all his hardness of mind, and of heart, he is dying of a fright. I heard it in the kitchen, I have heard it from himself,—he could not be deceived. If I had ever heard he was nervous, or fanciful, or superstitious, but a character so contrary to all these impressions;—a man that, as poor Butler says, in his 'Remains of the Antiquarian,' would have 'sold Christ over again for the numerical piece of silver which Judas got for him,'—such a man to die of fear! Yet he IS dying," said John, glancing his fearful eye on the contracted nostril, the glazed eye, the drooping jaw, the whole horrible apparatus of the facies Hippocraticae displayed, and soon to cease its display.

Old Melmoth at this moment seemed to be in a deep stupor; his eyes lost that little expression they had before, and his hands, that had convulsively been catching at the blankets, let go their short and quivering grasp, and lay extended on the bed like the claws of some bird that had died of hunger,—so meagre, so yellow, so spread. John, unaccustomed to the sight of death, believed this to be only a sign that he was going to sleep; and, urged by an impulse for which he did not attempt to account to himself, caught up the miserable light, and once more ventured into the forbidden room,— the BLUE CHAMBER of the dwelling. The motion roused the dying man;—he sat bolt upright in his bed. This John could not see, for he was now in the closet; but he heard the groan, or rather the choked and gurgling rattle of the throat, that announces the horrible conflict between muscular and mental convulsion. He started, turned away; but, as he turned away, he thought he saw the eyes of the portrait, on which his own was fixed, MOVE, and hurried back to his uncle's bedside.

Old Melmoth died in the course of that night, and died as he had lived, in a kind of avaricious delirium. John could not have imagined a scene so horrible as his last hours presented. He cursed and blasphemed about three halfpence, missing, as he said, some weeks before, in an account of change with his groom, about hay to a starved horse that he kept. Then he grasped John's hand, and asked him to give him the sacrament. "If I send to the clergyman, he will charge me something for it, which I cannot pay,— I cannot. They say I am rich,—look at this blanket;—but I would not mind that, if I could save my soul." And, raving, he added,

"Indeed, Doctor, I am a very poor man. I never troubled a clergyman before, and all I want is, that you will grant me two trifling requests, very little matters in your way,—save my soul, and (whispering) make interest to get me a parish coffin,—I have not enough left to bury me. I always told everyone I was poor, but the more I told them so, the less they believed me."

John, greatly shocked, retired from the bedside, and sat down in a distant corner of the room. The women were again in the room, which was very dark. Melmoth was silent from exhaustion, and there was a deathlike pause for some time. At this moment John saw the door open, and a figure appear at it, who looked round the room, and then quietly and deliberately retired, but not before John had discovered in his face the living original of the portrait. His first impulse was to utter an exclamation of terror, but his breath felt stopped. He was then rising to pursue the figure, but a moment's reflection checked him. What could be more absurd, than to be alarmed or amazed at a resemblance between a living man and the portrait of a dead one! The likeness was doubtless strong enough to strike him even in that darkened room, but it was doubtless only a likeness; and though it might be imposing enough to terrify an old man of gloomy and retired habits, and with a broken constitution, John resolved it should not produce the same effect on him.

But while he was applauding himself for this resolution, the door opened, and the figure appeared at it, beckoning and nodding to him, with a familiarity somewhat terrifying. John now started up, determined to pursue it; but the pursuit was stopped by the weak but shrill cries of his uncle, who was struggling at once with the agonies of death and his housekeeper. The poor woman, anxious for her master's reputation and her own, was trying to put on him a clean shirt and nightcap, and Melmoth, who had just sensation enough to perceive they were taking something from him, continued exclaiming feebly, "They are robbing me,—robbing me in my last moments,—robbing a dying man. John, won't you assist me,—I shall die a beggar; they are taking my last shirt,—I shall die a beggar."—And the miser died.

.　　.　　.　　.　　.　　.

A few days after the funeral, the will was opened before proper witnesses, and John was found to be left sole heir to his uncle's property, which, though originally moderate, had, by his grasping habits, and parsimonious life, become very considerable.

As the attorney who read the will concluded, he added, "There are some words here, at the corner of the parchment, which do not appear to be part of the will, as they are neither in the form of a codicil, nor is the signature of the testator affixed to them; but, to the best of my belief, they are in the handwriting of the deceased." As he spoke he showed the lines to Melmoth, who immediately recognized his uncle's hand (that perpendicular and penurious hand, that seems determined to make the most of the very paper, thriftily abridging every word, and leaving scarce an atom of margin), and read, not without some emotion, the following words: "I enjoin my nephew and heir, John Melmoth, to remove, destroy, or cause to be destroyed, the portrait inscribed J. Melmoth, 1646, hanging in my closet. I also enjoin him to search for a manuscript, which I think he will find in the third and lowest left-hand drawer of the mahogany chest standing under that portrait,—it is among some papers of no value, such as manuscript sermons, and pamphlets on the improvement of Ireland, and such stuff; he will distinguish it by its being tied round with a black tape, and the paper being very mouldy and discoloured. He may read it if he will;—I think he had better not. At all events, I adjure him, if there be any power in the adjuration of a dying man, to burn it."

After reading this singular memorandum, the business of the meeting was again resumed; and as old Melmoth's will was very clear and legally worded, all was soon settled, the party dispersed, and John Melmoth was left alone.

.　　.　　.　　.　　.　　.

He resolutely entered the closet, shut the door, and proceeded to search for the manuscript. It was soon found, for the directions of old Melmoth were forcibly written, and strongly remembered. The manuscript, old, tattered, and discoloured, was taken from the very drawer in which it was mentioned to be laid. Melmoth's hands felt as cold as those of his dead uncle, when he drew the blotted pages from their nook. He sat down to read,—there was a dead silence through the house. Melmoth looked wistfully at the candles, snuffed them, and still thought they looked dim, (perchance he thought they burned blue, but such thought he kept to himself). Certain it is, he often changed his posture, and would have changed his chair, had there been more than one in the apartment.

He sank for a few moments into a fit of gloomy abstraction, till the sound of the clock striking twelve made him start,—it was the only sound he had heard for some hours, and the sounds produced by inanimate things, while all living beings around are as dead, have at such an hour an effect indescribably awful. John looked at his manuscript with some reluctance, opened it, paused over the first lines, and as the wind sighed round the desolate apartment, and the rain pattered with a mournful sound against the dismantled window, wished—what did he wish for?—he wished the sound of the wind less dismal, and the dash of the rain less monotonous.—He may be forgiven, it was past midnight, and there was not a human being awake but himself within ten miles when he began to read.

.   .   .   .   .   .

The manuscript was discoloured, obliterated, and mutilated beyond any that had ever before exercised the patience of a reader. Michaelis himself, scrutinizing into the pretended autograph of St. Mark at Venice, never had a harder time of it.—Melmoth could make out only a sentence here and there. The writer, it appeared, was an Englishman of the name of Stanton, who had travelled abroad shortly after the Restoration. Travelling was not then attended with the facilities which modern improvement has introduced, and scholars and literati, the intelligent, the idle, and the curious, wandered over the Continent for years, like Tom Corvat, though they had the modesty, on their return, to entitle the result of their multiplied observations and labours only "crudities."

Stanton, about the year 1676, was in Spain; he was, like most of the travellers of that age, a man of literature, intelligence, and curiosity, but ignorant of the language of the country, and fighting his way at times from convent to convent, in quest of what was called "Hospitality," that is, obtaining board and lodging on the condition of holding a debate in Latin, on some point theological or metaphysical, with any monk who would become the champion of the strife. Now, as the theology was Catholic, and the metaphysics Aristotelian, Stanton sometimes wished himself at the miserable Posada from whose filth and famine he had been fighting his escape; but though his reverend antagonists always denounced his creed, and comforted themselves, even in defeat, with the assurance that he must be damned, on the double score of his being a heretic and an Englishman, they were obliged to confess that his Latin was good, and his logic unanswerable; and he was allowed, in most cases, to sup and sleep in peace. This was not doomed to be his fate on the night of the 17th August 1677, when he found himself in the plains of Valencia, deserted by a cowardly guide, who had been terrified by the sight of a cross erected as a memorial of a murder, had slipped off his mule unperceived, crossing himself every step he took on his retreat from the heretic, and left Stanton amid the terrors of an approaching storm, and the dangers of an unknown country. The sublime and yet softened beauty of the scenery around, had filled the soul of Stanton with delight, and he enjoyed that delight as Englishmen generally do, silently.

The magnificent remains of two dynasties that had passed away, the ruins of Roman palaces, and of Moorish fortresses, were around and above him;—the dark and heavy thunder clouds that advanced slowly, seemed like the shrouds of these spectres of departed greatness; they approached, but did not yet overwhelm or conceal them, as if Nature herself was for once awed by the power of man; and far below, the lovely valley of Valencia blushed and burned in all the glory of sunset, like a bride receiving the last glowing kiss of the bridegroom before the approach of night. Stanton gazed around. The difference between the architecture of the Roman and Moorish ruins struck him. Among the former are the remains of a theatre, and something like a public place; the latter present only the remains of fortresses, embattled, castellated, and fortified from top to bottom,—not a loophole for pleasure to get in by,—the loopholes were only for arrows; all denoted military power and despotic subjugation a l'outrance. The contrast might have pleased a philosopher, and he might have indulged in the reflection, that though the ancient Greeks and Romans were savages (as Dr. Johnson says all people who want a press must be, and he says truly), yet they were wonderful savages for their time, for they alone have left traces of their taste for pleasure in the countries they conquered, in their superb theatres, temples (which were also dedicated to pleasure one way or another), and baths, while other conquering bands of savages never left anything behind them but traces of their rage for power. So thought Stanton, as he still saw strongly defined, though darkened by the darkening clouds, the huge skeleton of a Roman amphitheatre, its arched and gigantic colonnades now admitting a gleam of light, and now commingling with the purple thunder cloud; and now the solid and heavy mass of a Moorish fortress, no light playing between its impermeable walls,— the image of power, dark, isolated, impenetrable. Stanton forgot his cowardly guide, his loneliness, his danger amid an approaching storm and an inhospitable country, where his name and country would shut every door against him, and every peal of thunder would be supposed justified by the daring intrusion of a heretic in the dwelling of an old Christian, as the Spanish Catholics absurdly term themselves, to mark the distinction between them and the baptized Moors.

All this was forgot in contemplating the glorious and awful scenery before him,—light struggling with darkness,—

and darkness menacing a light still more terrible, and announcing its menace in the blue and livid mass of cloud that hovered like a destroying angel in the air, its arrows aimed, but their direction awfully indefinite. But he ceased to forget these local and petty dangers, as the sublimity of romance would term them, when he saw the first flash of the lightning, broad and red as the banners of an insulting army whose motto is Vae victis, shatter to atoms the remains of a Roman tower;—the rifted stones rolled down the hill, and fell at the feet of Stanton. He stood appalled, and, awaiting his summons from the Power in whose eye pyramids, palaces, and the worms whose toil has formed them, and the worms who toil out their existence under their shadow or their pressure, are perhaps all alike contemptible, he stood collected, and for a moment felt that defiance of danger which danger itself excites, and we love to encounter it as a physical enemy, to bid it "do its worst," and feel that its worst will perhaps be ultimately its best for us. He stood and saw another flash dart its bright, brief, and malignant glance over the ruins of ancient power, and the luxuriance of recent fertility. Singular contrast! The relics of art forever decaying,—the productions of nature forever renewed.—(Alas! for what purpose are they renewed, better than to mock at the perishable monuments which men try in vain to rival them by.) The pyramids themselves must perish, but the grass that grows between their disjointed stones will be renewed from year to year.

Stanton was thinking thus, when all power of thought was suspended, by seeing two persons bearing between them the body of a young, and apparently very lovely girl, who had been struck dead by the lightning. Stanton approached, and heard the voices of the bearers repeating, "There is none who will mourn for her!" "There is none who will mourn for her!" said other voices, as two more bore in their arms the blasted and blackened figure of what had once been a man, comely and graceful;—"there is not ONE to mourn for her now!" They were lovers, and he had been consumed by the flash that had destroyed her, while in the act of endeavouring to defend her. As they were about to remove the bodies, a person approached with a calmness of step and demeanour, as if he were alone unconscious of danger, and incapable of fear; and after looking on them for some time, burst into a laugh so loud, wild, and protracted, that the peasants, starting with as much horror at the sound as at that of the storm, hurried away, bearing the corpses with them. Even Stanton's fears were subdued by his astonishment, and, turning to the stranger, who remained standing on the same spot, he asked the reason of such an outrage on humanity. The stranger, slowly turning round, and disclosing a countenance which—*(Here the manuscript was illegible for a few lines)*, said in English—*(A long hiatus followed here, and the next passage that was legible, though it proved to be a continuation of the narrative, was but a fragment.)*

.   .   .   .   .   .

The terrors of the night rendered Stanton a sturdy and unappeasable applicant; and the shrill voice of the old woman, repeating, "no heretic—no English—Mother of God protect us—avaunt Satan!"— combined with the clatter of the wooden casement (peculiar to the houses in Valencia) which she opened to discharge her volley of anathematization, and shut again as the lightning glanced through the aperture, were unable to repel his importunate request for admittance, in a night whose terrors ought to soften all the miserable petty local passions into one awful feeling of fear for the Power who caused it, and compassion for those who were exposed to it.—But Stanton felt there was something more than national bigotry in the exclamations of the old woman; there was a peculiar and personal horror of the English.—And he was right; but this did not diminish the eagerness of his. . . .

.   .   .   .   .   .

The house was handsome and spacious, but the melancholy appearance of desertion...

.   .   .   .   .   .

...The benches were by the wall, but there were none to sit there; the tables were spread in what had been the hall, but it seemed as if none had gathered round them for many years;—the clock struck audibly, there was no voice of mirth or of occupation to drown its sound; time told his awful lesson to silence alone;—the hearths were black with fuel long since consumed;—the family portraits looked as if they were the only tenants of the mansion; they seemed to say, from their mouldering frames, "there are none to gaze on us;" and the echo of the steps of Stanton and his feeble guide, was the only sound audible between the peals of thunder that rolled still awfully, but more distantly,—every peal like the exhausted murmurs of a spent heart. As they passed on, a shriek was heard. Stanton paused, and fearful images of the dangers to which travellers on the Continent are exposed in deserted and remote habitations, came into his mind. "Don't heed it," said the old woman, lighting him on with a miserable lamp;—"it is only he...

.   .   .   .   .   .

The old woman having now satisfied herself, by ocular demonstration, that her English guest, even if he was the devil, had neither horn, hoof, nor tail, that he could bear the sign of the cross without changing his form, and that, when he spoke, not a puff of sulphur came out of his mouth, began to take courage, and at length commenced her story, which, weary and comfortless as Stanton was, ...

.   .   .   .   .   .

Every obstacle was now removed; parents and relations at last gave up all opposition, and the young pair were united. Never was there a lovelier,—they seemed like angels who had only anticipated by a few years their celestial and eternal union. The marriage was solemnized with much pomp, and a few days after there was a feast in that very wainscoted chamber which you paused to remark was so gloomy. It was that night hung with rich tapestry, representing the exploits of the Cid, particularly that of his burning a few Moors who refused to renounce their accursed religion. They were represented beautifully tortured, writhing and howling, and "Mahomet! Mahomet!" issuing out of their mouths, as they called on him in their burning agonies;—you could almost hear them scream. At the upper end of the room, under a splendid estrade, over which was an image of the blessed Virgin, sat Donna Isabella de Cardoza, mother to the bride, and near her Donna Ines, the bride, on rich almohadas; the bridegroom sat opposite to her, and though they never spoke to each other, their eyes, slowly raised, but suddenly withdrawn (those eyes that blushed), told to each other the delicious secret of their happiness. Don Pedro de Cardoza had assembled a large party in honour of his daughter's nuptials; among them was an Englishman of the name of MELMOTH, a traveller; no one knew who had brought him there. He sat silent like the rest, while the iced waters and the sugared wafers were presented to the company. The night was intensely hot, and the moon glowed like a sun over the ruins of Saguntum; the embroidered blinds flapped heavily, as if the wind made an effort to raise them in vain, and then desisted.

(Another defect in the manuscript occurred here, but it was soon supplied.)

.   .   .   .   .   .

The company were dispersed through various alleys of the garden; the bridegroom and bride wandered through one where the delicious perfume of the orange trees mingled itself with that of the myrtles in blow. On their return to the ball, both of them asked, Had the company heard the exquisite sounds that floated through the garden just before they quitted it? No one had heard them. They expressed their surprise. The Englishman had never quitted the hall; it was said he smiled with a most particular and extraordinary expression as the remark was made. His silence had been noticed before, but it was ascribed to his ignorance of the Spanish language, an ignorance that Spaniards are not anxious either to expose or remove by speaking to a stranger. The subject of the music was not again reverted to till the guests were seated at supper, when Donna Ines and her young husband, exchanging a smile of delighted surprise, exclaimed they heard the same delicious sounds floating round them. The guests listened, but no one else could hear it;—everyone felt there was something extraordinary in this. Hush! was uttered by every voice almost at the same moment. A dead silence followed,—you would think, from their intent looks, that they listened with their very eyes. This deep silence, contrasted with the splendour of the feast, and the light effused from torches held by the domestics, produced a singular effect,—it seemed for some moments like an assembly of the dead. The silence was interrupted, though the cause of wonder had not ceased, by the entrance of Father Olavida, the Confessor of Donna Isabella, who had been called away previous to the feast, to administer extreme unction to a dying man in the neighbourhood. He was a priest of uncommon sanctity, beloved in the family, and respected in the neighbourhood, where he had displayed uncommon taste and talents for exorcism;—in fact, this was the good Father's forte, and he piqued himself on it accordingly. The devil never fell into worse hands than Father Olavida's, for when he was so contumacious as to resist Latin, and even the first verses of the Gospel of St. John in Greek, which the good Father never had recourse to but in cases of extreme stubbornness and difficulty,— (here Stanton recollected the English story of the Boy of Bilson, and blushed even in Spain for his countrymen),—then he always applied to the Inquisition; and if the devils were ever so obstinate before, they were always seen to fly out of the possessed, just as, in the midst of their cries (no doubt of blasphemy), they were tied to the stake. Some held out even till the flames surrounded them; but even the most stubborn must have been dislodged when the operation was over, for the devil himself could no longer tenant a crisp and glutinous lump of cinders. Thus Father Olavida's fame spread far and wide, and the Cardoza family had made uncommon interest to procure him for a Confessor, and happily succeeded. The ceremony he had just been performing had cast a shade over the good Father's countenance, but it dispersed as he mingled among the guests, and was introduced to them. Room was soon made for him, and he happened accidentally to be seated opposite the Englishman. As the wine was presented to him, Father Olavida (who, as I observed, was a man of singular sanctity) prepared to utter a short internal prayer. He hesitated,— trembled,—desisted; and, putting down the wine, wiped the drops from his forehead with the sleeve of his habit. Donna Isabella gave a sign to a domestic, and other wine of a higher quality was offered to him. His lips moved, as if in the effort to pronounce a benediction on it and the company, but the effort again failed; and the change in his countenance was so extraordinary, that it was perceived by all the guests. He felt the sensation that his extraordinary appearance excited, and attempted to remove it by again endeavouring to lift the cup to his lips. So strong was the anxiety with which the company watched him, that the only sound heard in that spacious and crowded hall was the rustling of his habit as he attempted to lift the cup to his lips once more—in vain. The guests sat in astonished silence. Father Olavida alone remained standing; but at that moment the Englishman rose, and appeared determined to fix Olavida's regards by a gaze like that of fascination. Olavida rocked, reeled, grasped the arm of a page, and at last, closing his eyes for a moment, as if to escape the horrible fascination of that unearthly glare (the Englishman's eyes were observed by all the guests, from the moment of his entrance, to effuse a most fearful and preternatural lustre), exclaimed, "Who is among us?—Who?—I cannot utter a blessing while he is here. I cannot feel one. Where he treads, the earth is parched!—Where he breathes, the air is fire!—Where he feeds, the food is poison!— Where he turns his glance is lightning!—WHO IS AMONG US?—WHO?" repeated the priest in the agony of adjuration, while his cowl fallen back, his few thin hairs around the scalp instinct and alive with terrible emotion, his outspread arms protruded from the sleeves of his habit, and extended toward the awful stranger, suggested the idea of an inspired being in the dreadful rapture of prophetic denunciation. He stood—still stood, and the Englishman stood calmly opposite to him. There was an agitated irregularity in the attitudes of those around them, which contrasted strongly the fixed and stern postures of those two, who remained gazing silently at each other. "Who knows him?" exclaimed Olavida, starting apparently from a trance; "who knows him? who brought him here?"

The guests severally disclaimed all knowledge of the Englishman, and each asked the other in whispers, "who HAD brought him there?" Father Olavida then pointed his arm to each of the company, and asked each individually, "Do you know him?" No! no! no!" was uttered with vehement emphasis by every individual. "But I know him," said Olavida, "by these cold drops!" and he wiped them off;— "by these convulsed joints!" and he attempted to sign the cross, but could not. He raised his voice, and evidently speaking with increased difficulty,—"By this bread and wine, which the faithful receive as the body and blood of Christ, but which HIS presence converts into matter as viperous as the suicide foam of the dying Judas,—by all these—I know him, and command him to be gone!—He is—he is—" and he bent forward as he spoke, and gazed on the Englishman with an expression which the mixture of rage, hatred, and fear rendered terrible. All the guests rose at these words,— the whole company now presented two singular groups, that of the amazed guests all collected together, and repeating, "Who, what is he?" and that of the Englishman, who stood unmoved, and Olavida, who dropped dead in the attitude of pointing to him.

.   .   .   .   .   .

The body was removed into another room, and the departure of the Englishman was not noticed till the company returned to the hall. They sat late together, conversing on this extraordinary circumstance, and finally agreed to remain in the house, lest the evil spirit (for they believed the Englishman no better) should take certain liberties with the corpse by no means agreeable to a Catholic, particularly as he had manifestly died without the benefit of the last sacraments. Just as this laudable resolution was formed, they were roused by cries of horror and agony from the bridal chamber, where the young pair had retired.

They hurried to the door, but the father was first. They burst it open, and found the bride a corpse in the arms of her husband.

. . . . . .

He never recovered his reason; the family deserted the mansion rendered terrible by so many misfortunes. One apartment is still tenanted by the unhappy maniac; his were the cries you heard as you traversed the deserted rooms. He is for the most part silent during the day, but at midnight he always exclaims, in a voice frightfully piercing, and hardly human, "They are coming! they are coming!" and relapses into profound silence.

The funeral of Father Olavida was attended by an extraordinary circumstance. He was interred in a neighbouring convent; and the reputation of his sanctity, joined to the interest caused by his extraordinary death, collected vast numbers at the ceremony. His funeral sermon was preached by a monk of distinguished eloquence, appointed for the purpose. To render the effect of his discourse more powerful, the corpse, extended on a bier, with its face uncovered, was placed in the aisle. The monk took his text from one of the prophets,—"Death is gone up into our palaces." He expatiated on mortality, whose approach, whether abrupt or lingering, is alike awful to man.—He spoke of the vicissitudes of empires with much eloquence and learning, but his audience were not observed to be much affected.—He cited various passages from the lives of the saints, descriptive of the glories of martyrdom, and the heroism of those who had bled and blazed for Christ and his blessed mother, but they appeared still waiting for something to touch them more deeply. When he inveighed against the tyrants under whose bloody persecution those holy men suffered, his hearers were roused for a moment, for it is always easier to excite a passion than a moral feeling. But when he spoke of the dead, and pointed with emphatic gesture to the corpse, as it lay before them cold and motionless, every eye was fixed, and every ear became attentive. Even the lovers, who, under pretence of dipping

32

their fingers into the holy water, were contriving to exchange amorous billets, forbore for one moment this interesting intercourse, to listen to the preacher. He dwelt with much energy on the virtues of the deceased, whom he declared to be a particular favourite of the Virgin; and enumerating the various losses that would be caused by his departure to the community to which he belonged, to society, and to religion at large; he at last worked up himself to a vehement expostulation with the Deity on the occasion. "Why hast thou," he exclaimed, "why hast thou, Oh God! thus dealt with us? Why hast thou snatched from our sight this glorious saint, whose merits, if properly applied, doubtless would have been sufficient to atone for the apostasy of St. Peter, the opposition of St. Paul (previous to his conversion), and even the treachery of Judas himself? Why hast thou, Oh God! snatched him from us?"—and a deep and hollow voice from among the congregation answered,—"Because he deserved his fate." The murmurs of approbation with which the congregation honoured this apostrophe half drowned this extraordinary interruption; and though there was some little commotion in the immediate vicinity of the speaker, the rest of the audience continued to listen intently. "What," proceeded the preacher, pointing to the corpse, "what hath laid thee there, servant of God?"—"Pride, ignorance, and fear," answered the same voice, in accents still more thrilling. The disturbance now became universal. The preacher paused, and a circle opening, disclosed the figure of a monk belonging to the convent, who stood among them.

.   .   .   .   .   .

After all the usual modes of admonition, exhortation, and discipline had been employed, and the bishop of the diocese, who, under the report of these extraordinary circumstances, had visited the convent in person to obtain some explanation from the contumacious monk in vain, it was agreed, in a chapter extraordinary, to surrender him to the power of the Inquisition. He testified great horror when this determination was made known to him,—and offered to tell over and over again all that he COULD relate of the cause of Father Olavida's death. His humiliation, and repeated offers of confession, came too late. He was conveyed to the Inquisition. The proceedings of that tribunal are rarely disclosed, but there is a secret report (I cannot answer for its truth) of what he said and suffered there. On his first examination, he said he would relate all he COULD. He was told that was not enough, he must relate all he knew.

.   .   .   .   .   .

"Why did you testify such horror at the funeral of Father Olavida?"—"Everyone testified horror and grief at the death of that venerable ecclesiastic, who died in the door of sanctity. Had I done otherwise, it might have been reckoned a proof of my guilt." "Why did you interrupt the preacher with such extraordinary exclamations?"—To this no answer. "Why do you refuse to explain the meaning of those exclamations?"—No answer. "Why do you persist in this obstinate and dangerous silence? Look, I beseech you, brother, at the cross that is suspended against this wall," and the Inquisitor pointed to the large black crucifix at the back of the chair where he sat; "one drop of the blood shed there can purify you from all the sin you have ever committed; but all that blood, combined with the intercession of the Queen of Heaven, and the merits of all its martyrs, nay, even the absolution of the Pope, cannot deliver you from the curse of dying in unrepented sin."—"What sin, then, have I committed?"—"The greatest of all possible sins; you refuse answering the questions put to you at the tribunal of the most holy and merciful Inquisition;—you will not tell us what you know concerning the death of Father Olavida."—"I have told you that I believe he perished in consequence of his ignorance and presumption." "What proof can you produce of that?"— "He sought the knowledge of a secret withheld from man." "What was that?"—"The secret of discovering the presence or agency of the evil power." "Do you possess that secret?"—After much agitation on the part of the prisoner, he said distinctly, but very faintly, "My master forbids me to disclose it." "If your master were Jesus Christ, he would not forbid you to obey the commands, or answer the questions of

34

the Inquisition."—"I am not sure of that." There was a general outcry of horror at these words. The examination then went on. "If you believed Olavida to be guilty of any pursuits or studies condemned by our mother the church, why did you not denounce him to the Inquisition?"—"Because I believed him not likely to be injured by such pursuits; his mind was too weak,— he died in the struggle," said the prisoner with great emphasis. "You believe, then, it requires strength of mind to keep those abominable secrets, when examined as to their nature and tendency?"—"No, I rather imagine strength of body." "We shall try that presently," said an Inquisitor, giving a signal for the torture.

.   .   .   .   .   .

The prisoner underwent the first and second applications with unshrinking courage, but on the infliction of the water-torture, which is indeed insupportable to humanity, either to suffer or relate, he exclaimed in the gasping interval, he would disclose everything. He was released, refreshed, restored, and the following day uttered the following remarkable confession...

.   .   .   .   .   .

The old Spanish woman further confessed to Stanton, that...

.   .   .   .   .   .

...and that the Englishman certainly had been seen in the neighbourhood since;—seen, as she had heard, that very night. "Great G—d!" exclaimed Stanton, as he recollected the stranger whose demoniac laugh had so appalled him, while gazing on the lifeless bodies of the lovers, whom the lightning had struck and blasted.

As the manuscript, after a few blotted and illegible pages, became more distinct, Melmoth read on, perplexed and unsatisfied, not knowing what connection this Spanish story could have with his ancestor, whom, however, he recognized under the title of the Englishman; and wondering how Stanton could have thought it worth his while to follow him to Ireland, write a long manuscript about an event that occurred in Spain, and leave it in the hands of his family, to "verify untrue things," in the language of Dogberry,— his wonder was diminished, though his curiosity was still more inflamed, by the perusal of the next lines, which he made out with some difficulty. It seems Stanton was now in England.

. . . . . .

About the year 1677, Stanton was in London, his mind still full of his mysterious countryman. This constant subject of his contemplations had produced a visible change in his exterior,—his walk was what Sallust tells us of Catiline's,— his were, too, the "faedi oculi." He said to himself every moment, "If I could but trace that being, I will not call him man,"—and the next moment he said, "and what if I could?" In this state of mind, it is singular enough that he mixed constantly in public amusements, but it is true. When one fierce passion is devouring the soul, we feel more than ever the necessity of external excitement; and our dependence on the world for temporary relief increases in direct proportion to our contempt of the world and all its works. He went frequently to the theatres, THEN fashionable, when

"The fair sat panting at a courtier's play,
    And not a mask went unimproved away."

. . . . . .

It was that memorable night, when, according to the history of the veteran Betterton,* Mrs. Barry, who personated Roxana, had a green-room squabble with Mrs. Bowtell, the representative of Statira, about a veil, which the partiality of the property man adjudged to the latter. Roxana suppressed her rage till the fifth act, when, stabbing Statira, she aimed the blow with such force as to pierce through her stays, and inflict a severe though not dangerous wound. Mrs. Bowtell fainted, the performance was suspended, and, in the commotion which this incident caused in the house, many of the audience rose, and Stanton among them. It was at this moment that, in a seat opposite to him, he discovered the

---

* Vide Betterton's History of the Stage.

object of his search for four years,—the Englishman whom he had met in the plains of Valencia, and whom he believed the same with the subject of the extraordinary narrative he had heard there.

He was standing up. There was nothing particular or remarkable in his appearance, but the expression of his eyes could never be mistaken or forgotten. The heart of Stanton palpitated with violence,—a mist overspread his eye,—a nameless and deadly sickness, accompanied with a creeping sensation in every pore, from which cold drops were gushing, announced the...

   .   .   .   .   .   .

Before he had well recovered, a strain of music, soft, solemn, and delicious, breathed round him, audibly ascending from the ground, and increasing in sweetness and power till it seemed to fill the whole building. Under the sudden impulse of amazement and pleasure, he inquired of some around him from whence those exquisite sounds arose. But, by the manner in which he was answered, it was plain that those he addressed considered him insane; and, indeed, the remarkable change in his expression might well justify the suspicion. He then remembered that night in Spain, when the same sweet and mysterious sounds were heard only by the young bridegroom and bride, of whom the latter perished on that very night. "And am I then to be the next victim?" thought Stanton; "and are those celestial sounds, that seem to prepare us for heaven, only intended to announce the presence of an incarnate fiend, who mocks the devoted with 'airs from heaven,' while he prepares to surround them with 'blasts from hell'?" It is very singular that at this moment, when his imagination had reached its highest pitch of elevation,—when the object he had pursued so long and fruitlessly, had in one moment become as it were tangible to the grasp both of mind and body,—when this spirit, with whom he had wrestled in darkness, was at last about to declare its name, that Stanton began to feel a kind of disappointment at the futility of his pursuits, like Bruce at discovering the source of the Nile, or Gibbon on concluding his History. The feeling which he had dwelt on so long, that he had actually converted it into a duty, was after all mere curiosity; but what passion is more insatiable, or more capable of giving a kind of romantic grandeur to all its wanderings and eccentricities? Curiosity is in one respect like love, it always compromises between the object and the feeling; and provided the latter possesses sufficient energy, no matter how contemptible the former may be. A child might have smiled at the agitation of Stanton, caused as it was by the accidental appearance of a stranger; but no man, in the full energy of his passions, was there, but must have trembled at the horrible agony of emotion with which he felt approaching, with sudden and irresistible velocity, the crisis of his destiny.

When the play was over, he stood for some moments in the deserted streets. It was a beautiful moonlight night, and he saw near him a figure, whose shadow, projected half across the street (there were no flagged ways then, chains and posts were the only defence of the foot passenger), appeared to him of gigantic magnitude. He had been so long accustomed to contend with these phantoms of the imagination, that he took a kind of stubborn delight in subduing them. He walked up to the object, and observing the shadow only was magnified, and the figure was the ordinary height of man, he approached it, and discovered the very object of his search,—the man whom he had seen for a moment in Valencia, and, after a search of four years, recognized at the theatre.

.   .   .   .   .   .

"You were in quest of me?"—"I was." "Have you anything to inquire of me?"—"Much." "Speak, then."—"This is no place." "No place! poor wretch, I am independent of time and place. Speak, if you have anything to ask or to learn."— "I have many things to ask, but nothing to learn, I hope, from you." "You deceive yourself, but you will be undeceived when next we meet."—"And when shall that be?" said Stanton, grasping his arm; "name your hour and your place." "The hour shall be midday," answered the stranger, with a horrid and unintelligible smile; "and the place shall be the bare walls of a madhouse, where you shall rise rattling in your chains, and rustling from your straw, to greet me,—yet still you shall have THE CURSE OF SANITY, and of memory. My voice shall ring in your ears till then, and the glance of these eyes shall be reflected from every object, animate or inanimate, till you behold them again."—"Is it under circumstances so horrible we are to meet again?" said Stanton, shrinking under the full-lighted blaze of those demon eyes. "I never," said the stranger, in an emphatic tone,—"I never desert my friends in misfortune. When they are plunged in the lowest abyss of human calamity, they are sure to be visited by me."

. . . . . .

The narrative, when Melmoth was again able to trace its continuation, described Stanton, some years after, plunged in a state the most deplorable.

He had been always reckoned of a singular turn of mind, and the belief of this, aggravated by his constant talk of Melmoth, his wild pursuit of him, his strange behaviour at the theatre, and his dwelling on the various particulars of their extraordinary meetings, with all the intensity of the deepest conviction (while he never could impress them on any one's conviction but his own), suggested to some prudent people the idea that he was deranged. Their malignity probably took part with their prudence. The selfish Frenchman[†] says, we feel a pleasure even in the misfortunes of our friends,—a plus forte in those of our enemies; and as everyone is an enemy to a man of genius of course, the report of Stanton's malady was propagated with infernal and successful industry. Stanton's next relative, a needy unprincipled man, watched the report in its circulation, and saw the snares closing round his victim. He waited on him one morning, accompanied by a person of a grave, though somewhat repulsive appearance. Stanton was as usual abstracted and restless, and, after a few moments'

[†] Rochefoucauld.

conversation, he proposed a drive a few miles out of London, which he said would revive and refresh him. Stanton objected, on account of the difficulty of getting a hackney coach (for it is singular that at this period the number of private equipages, though infinitely fewer than they are now, exceeded the number of hired ones), and proposed going by water. This, however, did not suit the kinsman's views; and, after pretending to send for a carriage (which was in waiting at the end of the street), Stanton and his companions entered it, and drove about two miles out of London.

The carriage then stopped. Come, Cousin," said the younger Stanton,—"come and view a purchase I have made." Stanton absently alighted, and followed him across a small paved court; the other person followed. "In troth, Cousin," said Stanton, "your choice appears not to have been discreetly made; your house has somewhat of a gloomy aspect."—"Hold you content, Cousin," replied the other; "I shall take order that you like it better, when you have been some time a dweller therein." Some attendants of a mean appearance, and with most suspicious visages, awaited them on their entrance, and they ascended a narrow staircase, which led to a room meanly furnished. "Wait here," said the kinsman, to the man who accompanied them, "till I go for company to divertise my cousin in his loneliness." They were left alone. Stanton took no notice of his companion, but as usual seized the first book near him, and began to read. It was a volume in manuscript,—they were then much more common than now.

The first lines struck him as indicating insanity in the writer. It was a wild proposal (written apparently after the great fire of London) to rebuild it with stone, and attempting to prove, on a calculation wild, false, and yet sometimes plausible, that this could be done out of the colossal fragments of Stonehenge, which the writer proposed to remove for that purpose. Subjoined were several grotesque drawings of engines designed to remove those massive blocks, and in a corner of the page was a note,—"I would have drawn these more accurately, but was not allowed a KNIFE to mend my pen."

The next was entitled, "A modest proposal for the spreading of Christianity in foreign parts, whereby it is hoped its entertainment will become general all over the world."—This modest proposal was, to convert the Turkish ambassadors (who had been in London a few years before), by offering them their choice of being strangled on the spot, or becoming Christians. Of course the writer reckoned on their embracing the easier alternative, but even this was to be clogged with a heavy condition,—namely, that they must be bound before a magistrate to convert twenty Mussulmans a day, on their return to Turkey. The rest of the pamphlet was reasoned very much in the conclusive style of Captain Bobadil,— these twenty will convert twenty more apiece, and these two hundred converts, converting their due number in the same time, all Turkey would be converted before the Grand Seignior knew where he was. Then comes the coup d'eclat,—one fine morning, every minaret in Constantinople was to ring out with bells, instead of the cry of the Muezzins; and the Imaum, coming out to see what was the matter, was to be encountered by the Archbishop of Canterbury, in pontificalibus, performing Cathedral service in the church of St. Sophia, which was to finish the business. Here an objection appeared to arise, which the ingenuity of the writer had anticipated.—"It may be redargued," saith he, "by those who have more spleen than brain, that forasmuch as the Archbishop preacheth in English, he will not thereby much edify the Turkish folk, who do altogether hold in a vain gabble of their own." But this (to use his own language) he "evites," by judiciously observing, that where service was performed in an unknown tongue, the devotion of the people was always observed to be much increased thereby; as, for instance, in the church of Rome,—that St. Augustine, with his monks, advanced to meet King Ethelbert singing litanies (in a language his majesty could not possibly have understood), and converted him and his whole court on the spot;—that the sibylline books...

41

. . . . . .

Cum multis aliis.

Between the pages were cut most exquisitely in paper the likenesses of some of these Turkish ambassadors; the hair of the beards, in particular, was feathered with a delicacy of touch that seemed the work of fairy fingers,—but the pages ended with a complaint of the operator, that his scissors had been taken from him. However, he consoled himself and the reader with the assurance, that he would that night catch a moonbeam as it entered through the grating, and, when he had whetted it on the iron knobs of his door, would do wonders with it. In the next page was found a melancholy proof of powerful but prostrated intellect. It contained some insane lines, ascribed to Lee the dramatic poet, commencing,

"O that my lungs could bleat like buttered pease," &c.

There is no proof whatever that these miserable lines were really written by Lee, except that the measure is the fashionable quatrain of the period. It is singular that Stanton read on without suspicion of his own danger, quite absorbed in the album of a madhouse, without ever reflecting on the place where he was, and which such compositions too manifestly designated.

It was after a long interval that he looked round, and perceived that his companion was gone. Bells were unusual then. He proceeded to the door,—it was fastened. He called aloud,—his voice was echoed in a moment by many others, but in tones so wild and discordant, that he desisted in involuntary terror. As the day advanced, and no one approached, he tried the window, and then perceived for the first time it was grated. It looked out on the narrow flagged yard, in which no human being was; and if there had, from such a being no human feeling could have been extracted.

Sickening with unspeakable horror, he sunk rather than sat down beside the miserable window, and "wished for day."

.   .   .   .   .   .

At midnight he started from a doze, half a swoon, half a sleep, which probably the hardness of his seat, and of the deal table on which he leaned, had not contributed to prolong.

He was in complete darkness; the horror of his situation struck him at once, and for a moment he was indeed almost qualified for an inmate of that dreadful mansion. He felt his way to the door, shook it with desperate strength, and uttered the most frightful cries, mixed with expostulations and commands. His cries were in a moment echoed by a hundred voices. In maniacs there is a peculiar malignity, accompanied by an extraordinary acuteness of some of the senses, particularly in distinguishing the voice of a stranger. The cries that he heard on every side seemed like a wild and infernal yell of joy, that their mansion of misery had obtained another tenant.

He paused, exhausted,—a quick and thundering step was heard in the passage. The door was opened, and a man of savage appearance stood at the entrance,—two more were seen indistinctly in the passage. "Release me, villain!"—"Stop, my fine fellow, what's all this noise for?" "Where am I?" "Where you ought to be." "Will you dare to detain me?"—"Yes, and a little more than that," answered the ruffian, applying a loaded horsewhip to his back and shoulders, till the patient soon fell to the ground convulsed with rage and pain. "Now you see you are where you ought to be," repeated the ruffian, brandishing the horsewhip over him, "and now take the advice of a friend, and make no more noise. The lads are ready for you with the darbies, and they'll clink them on in the crack of this whip, unless you prefer another touch of it first." They then were advancing into the room as he spoke, with fetters in their hands (strait waistcoats being then little known or used), and showed, by their frightful countenances and gestures, no unwillingness to apply them. Their harsh rattle on the stone pavement made Stanton's blood run cold; the effect, however, was useful. He had the presence of mind to acknowledge his (supposed) miserable condition, to supplicate the forbearance of the ruthless keeper, and promise complete submission to his orders. This pacified the ruffian, and he retired.

Stanton collected all his resolution to encounter the horrible night; he saw all that was before him, and summoned himself to meet it. After much agitated deliberation, he conceived it best to continue the same appearance of submission and tranquillity, hoping that thus he might in time either propitiate the wretches in whose hands he was, or, by his apparent inoffensiveness, procure such opportunities of indulgence, as might perhaps ultimately facilitate his escape. He therefore determined to conduct himself with the utmost tranquillity, and never to let his voice be heard in the house; and he laid down several other resolutions with a degree of prudence which he already shuddered to think might be the cunning of incipient madness, or the beginning result of the horrid habits of the place.

These resolutions were put to desperate trial that very night. Just next to Stanton's apartment were lodged two most uncongenial neighbours. One of them was a puritanical weaver, who had been driven mad by a single sermon from the celebrated Hugh Peters, and was sent to the madhouse as full of election and reprobation as he could hold,—and fuller. He regularly repeated over the five points while daylight lasted, and imagined himself preaching in a conventicle with distinguished success; toward twilight his visions were more gloomy, and at midnight his blasphemies became horrible. In the opposite cell was lodged a loyalist tailor, who had been ruined by giving credit to the cavaliers and their ladies,—(for at this time, and much later, down to the reign of Anne, tailors were employed by females even to make and fit on their stays),—who had run mad with drink and loyalty on the burning of the Rump, and ever since had made the cells of the madhouse echo with fragments of the ill-fated Colonel Lovelace's song, scraps from Cowley's "Cutter of Coleman street," and some curious specimens from Mrs. Aphra Behn's plays, where the cavaliers are denominated the heroicks, and Lady Lambert and Lady Desborough represented as going to meeting, their large Bibles carried before them by their pages, and falling in love with two banished cavaliers by the way. The voice in which he shrieked out such words was powerfully horrible, but it was like the moan of an infant compared to the voice which took up and re-echoed the cry, in a tone that made the building shake. It was the voice of a maniac, who had lost her husband, children, subsistence, and finally her reason, in the dreadful fire of London. The cry of fire never failed to operate with terrible punctuality on her associations. She had been in a disturbed sleep, and now started from it as suddenly as on that dreadful night. It was Saturday night too, and she was always observed to be particularly violent on that night,—it was the terrible weekly festival of insanity with her. She was awake, and busy in a moment escaping from the flames; and she dramatized the whole scene with such hideous fidelity, that Stanton's resolution was far more in danger from her than from the battle between his neighbours Testimony and Hothead. She began exclaiming she was suffocated by the smoke; then she sprung from her bed, calling for a light, and appeared to be struck by the sudden glare that burst through her casement.—"The last day," she shrieked, "The last day! The very heavens are on fire!"— "That will not come till the Man of Sin be first destroyed," cried the weaver; "thou ravest of light and fire, and yet thou art in utter darkness.—I pity thee, poor mad soul, I pity thee!" The maniac never heeded him; she appeared to be scrambling up a staircase to her children's room. She exclaimed she was scorched, singed, suffocated; her courage appeared to fail, and she retreated. "But my children are there!" she cried in a voice of unspeakable agony, as she seemed to make another effort; "here I am—here I am come to save you.—Oh God! They are all blazing!—Take this arm—no, not that, it is scorched and disabled— well, any arm—take hold of my clothes—no, they are blazing too!— Well, take me all on fire as I am!—And their hair, how it hisses!—Water, one drop of water for my youngest—he is but an infant—for my youngest, and let me burn!" She paused in

45

horrid silence, to watch the fall of a blazing rafter that was about to shatter the staircase on which she stood.—"The roof has fallen on my head!" she exclaimed. "The earth is weak, and all the inhabitants thereof," chanted the weaver; "I bear up the pillars of it."

The maniac marked the destruction of the spot where she thought she stood by one desperate bound, accompanied by a wild shriek, and then calmly gazed on her infants as they rolled over the scorching fragments, and sunk into the abyss of fire below. "There they go,— one—two—three—all!" and her voice sunk into low mutterings, and her convulsions into faint, cold shudderings, like the sobbings of a spent storm, as she imagined herself to "stand in safety and despair," amid the thousand houseless wretches assembled in the suburbs of London on the dreadful nights after the fire, without food, roof, or raiment, all gazing on the burning ruins of their dwellings and their property. She seemed to listen to their complaints, and even repeated some of them very affectingly, but invariably answered them with the same words, "But I have lost all my children—all!" It was remarkable, that when this sufferer began to rave, all the others became silent. The cry of nature hushed every other cry,—she was the only patient in the house who was not mad from politics, religion, ebriety, or some perverted passion; and terrifying as the outbreak of her frenzy always was, Stanton used to await it as a kind of relief from the dissonant, melancholy, and ludicrous ravings of the others.

But the utmost efforts of his resolution began to sink under the continued horrors of the place. The impression on his senses began to defy the power of reason to resist them. He could not shut out these frightful cries nightly repeated, nor the frightful sound of the whip employed to still them. Hope began to fail him, as he observed, that the submissive tranquillity (which he had imagined, by obtaining increased indulgence, might contribute to his escape, or perhaps convince the keeper of his sanity) was interpreted by the callous ruffian, who was acquainted only with the varieties of

MADNESS, as a more refined species of that cunning which he was well accustomed to watch and baffle.

On his first discovery of his situation, he had determined to take the utmost care of his health and intellect that the place allowed, as the sole basis of his hope of deliverance. But as that hope declined, he neglected the means of realizing it. He had at first risen early, walked incessantly about his cell, and availed himself of every opportunity of being in the open air. He took the strictest care of his person in point of cleanliness, and with or without appetite, regularly forced down his miserable meals; and all these efforts were even pleasant, as long as hope prompted them. But now he began to relax them all. He passed half the day in his wretched bed, in which he frequently took his meals, declined shaving or changing his linen, and, when the sun shone into his cell, he turned from it on his straw with a sigh of heartbroken despondency. Formerly, when the air breathed through his grating, he used to say, "Blessed air of heaven, I shall breathe you once more in freedom!—Reserve all your freshness for that delicious evening when I shall inhale you, and be as free as you myself." Now when he felt it, he sighed and said nothing. The twitter of the sparrows, the pattering of rain, or the moan of the wind, sounds that he used to sit up in his bed to catch with delight, as reminding him of nature, were now unheeded.

He began at times to listen with sullen and horrible pleasure to the cries of his miserable companions. He became squalid, listless, torpid, and disgusting in his appearance.

.   .   .   .   .   .

It was one of those dismal nights, that, as he tossed on his loathsome bed,—more loathsome from the impossibility to quit it without feeling more "unrest,"—he perceived the miserable light that burned in the hearth was obscured by the intervention of some dark object. He turned feebly toward the light, without curiosity, without excitement, but with a wish to diversify the monotony of his misery, by observing the slightest change made even accidentally in the dusky atmosphere of his cell. Between him and the light stood the figure of Melmoth, just as he had seen him from the first; the figure was the same; the expression of the face was the same,—cold, stony, and rigid; the eyes, with their infernal and dazzling lustre, were still the same.

Stanton's ruling passion rushed on his soul; he felt this apparition like a summons to a high and fearful encounter. He heard his heart beat audibly, and could have exclaimed with Lee's unfortunate heroine,—"It pants as cowards do before a battle; Oh the great march has sounded!"

Melmoth approached him with that frightful calmness that mocks the terror it excites. "My prophecy has been fulfilled;—you rise to meet me rattling from your chains, and rustling from your straw—am I not a true prophet?" Stanton was silent. "Is not your situation very miserable?"—Still Stanton was silent; for he was beginning to believe this an illusion of madness. He thought to himself, "How could he have gained entrance here?"—"Would you not wish to be delivered from it?" Stanton tossed on his straw, and its rustling seemed to answer the question. "I have the power to deliver you from it." Melmoth spoke very slowly and very softly, and the melodious smoothness of his voice made a frightful contrast to the stony rigor of his features, and the fiendlike brilliancy of his eyes. "Who are you, and whence come you?" said Stanton, in a tone that was meant to be interrogatory and imperative, but which, from his habits of squalid debility, was at once feeble and querulous. His intellect had become affected by the gloom of his miserable habitation, as the wretched inmate of a similar mansion, when produced before a medical examiner, was reported to be a complete Albino.—His skin was bleached, his eyes turned white; he could not bear the light; and, when exposed to it, he turned away with a mixture of weakness and restlessness, more like the writhings of a sick infant than the struggles of a man.

Such was Stanton's situation. He was enfeebled now, and the power of the enemy seemed without a possibility of opposition from either his intellectual or corporeal powers.

.   .   .   .   .

Of all their horrible dialogue, only these words were legible in the manuscript, "You know me now."—"I always knew you."—"That is false; you imagined you did, and that has been the cause of all the wild, of the.. ...of your finally being lodged in this mansion of misery, where only I would seek, where only I can succour you."—"You, demon!"— "Demon!—Harsh words!—Was it a demon or a human being placed you here?—Listen to me, Stanton; nay, wrap not yourself in that miserable blanket,—that cannot shut out my words. Believe me, were you folded in thunder clouds, you must hear ME! Stanton, think of your misery. These bare walls—what do they present to the intellect or to the senses?—Whitewash, diversified with the scrawls of charcoal or red chalk, that your happy predecessors have left for you to trace over. You have a taste for drawing—I trust it will improve. And here's a grating, through which the sun squints on you like a stepdame, and the breeze blows, as if it meant to tantalize you with a sigh from that sweet mouth, whose kiss you must never enjoy. And where's your library,— intellectual man,—travelled man?" he repeated in a tone of bitter derision; "where be your companions, your peaked men of countries, as your favourite Shakespeare has it? You must be content with the spider and the rat, to crawl and scratch round your flock bed! I have known prisoners in the Bastille to feed them for companions,—why don't you begin your task? I have known a spider to descend at the tap of a finger, and a rat to come forth when the daily meal was brought, to share it with his fellow prisoner!—How delightful to have vermin for your guests! Aye, and when the feast fails them, they make a meal of their entertainer!—You shudder.—Are you, then, the first prisoner who has been devoured alive by the vermin that infested his cell?—Delightful banquet, not 'where you eat, but where you are eaten'! Your guests, however, will give you one token of repentance while they feed; there will be gnashing of teeth, and you shall hear it, and feel it too perchance!—And then for meals—Oh you are daintily off!—The soup that the cat has lapped; and (as her progeny has probably contributed to the hell broth) why not? Then your hours of solitude, deliciously diversified by the yell of famine, the howl of madness, the crash of whips, and the broken-hearted sob of those who, like you, are supposed, or DRIVEN mad by the crimes of others!—Stanton, do you imagine your reason can possibly hold out amid such scenes?— Supposing your reason was unimpaired, your health not destroyed,— suppose all this, which is, after all, more than fair supposition can grant, guess the effect of the continuance of these scenes on your senses alone. A time will come, and soon, when, from mere habit, you will echo the scream of every delirious wretch that harbours near you; then you will pause, clasp your hands on your throbbing head, and listen with horrible anxiety whether the scream proceeded from YOU or THEM. The time will come, when, from the want of occupation, the listless and horrible vacancy of your hours, you will feel as anxious to hear those shrieks, as you were at first terrified to hear them,—when you will watch for the ravings of your next neighbour, as you would for a scene on the stage. All humanity will be extinguished in you. The ravings of these wretches will become at once your sport and your torture. You will watch for the sounds, to mock them with the grimaces and bellowings of a fiend. The mind has a power of accommodating itself to its situation, that you will experience in its most frightful and deplorable efficacy. Then comes the dreadful doubt of one's own sanity, the terrible announcer that THAT doubt will soon become fear, and THAT fear certainty. Perhaps (still more dreadful) the FEAR will at last become a HOPE,—shut out from society, watched by a brutal keeper, writhing with all the impotent agony of an incarcerated mind, without communication and without sympathy, unable to exchange ideas but with those whose ideas are only the hideous spectres of departed intellect, or even to hear the welcome sound of the human voice, except to mistake it for the howl of a fiend, and stop the ear desecrated by its intrusion,— then at last your fear will become a more fearful hope; you will wish to become one of them, to escape the agony of consciousness. As those who have long leaned over a precipice, have at last felt a desire to plunge below, to relieve the intolerable temptation of their giddiness,‡ you will hear them laugh amid their wildest paroxysms; you will say, 'Doubtless those wretches have some consolation, but I have none; my sanity is my greatest curse in this abode of horrors. They greedily devour their miserable meals, while I loathe mine. They sleep sometimes soundly, while my sleep is— worse than their waking. They are revived every morning by some delicious illusion of cunning madness, soothing them with the hope of escaping, baffling or tormenting their keeper; my sanity precludes all such hope. I KNOW I NEVER CAN ESCAPE, and the preservation of my faculties is only an aggravation of my sufferings. I have all their miseries,—I have none of their consolations. They laugh,—I hear them; would I could laugh like them.' You will try, and the very effort will be an invocation to the demon of insanity to come and take full possession of you from that moment forever."

(There were other details, both of the menaces and temptations employed by Melmoth, which are too horrible for insertion. One of them may serve for an instance.)

"You think that the intellectual power is something distinct from the vitality of the soul, or, in other words, that if even your reason should be destroyed (which it nearly is), your soul might yet enjoy beatitude in the full exercise of its enlarged and exalted faculties, and all the clouds which obscured them be dispelled by the Sun of Righteousness, in whose beams you hope to bask forever and ever. Now, without going into any metaphysical subtleties about the distinction between mind and soul, experience must teach you, that there can be no crime into which madmen would not, and do not, precipitate themselves; mischief is their occupation, malice their habit, murder their sport, and blasphemy their delight. Whether a soul in this state can be

---

‡ A fact, related to me by a person who was near committing suicide in a similar situation, to escape what he called "the excruciating torture of giddiness."

51

in a hopeful one, it is for you to judge; but it seems to me, that with the loss of reason (and reason cannot long be retained in this place) you lose also the hope of immortality.—Listen," said the tempter, pausing, "listen to the wretch who is raving near you, and whose blasphemies might make a demon start.—He was once an eminent puritanical preacher. Half the day he imagines himself in a pulpit, denouncing damnation against Papists, Arminians, and even Sublapsarians (he being a Supra-lapsarian himself). He foams, he writhes, he gnashes his teeth; you would imagine him in the hell he was painting, and that the fire and brimstone he is so lavish of were actually exhaling from his jaws. At night his creed retaliates on him; he believes himself one of the reprobates he has been all day denouncing, and curses God for the very decree he has all day been glorifying Him for.

"He, whom he has for twelve hours been vociferating 'is the loveliest among ten thousand,' becomes the object of demoniac hostility and execration. He grapples with the iron posts of his bed, and says he is rooting out the cross from the very foundations of Calvary; and it is remarkable, that in proportion as his morning exercises are intense, vivid, and eloquent, his nightly blasphemies are outrageous and horrible.—Hark! Now he believes himself a demon; listen to his diabolical eloquence of horror!"

Stanton listened, and shuddered...

.   .   .   .   .   .

"Escape—escape for your life," cried the tempter; "break forth into life, liberty, and sanity. Your social happiness, your intellectual powers, your immortal interests, perhaps, depend on the choice of this moment.—There is the door, and the key is in my hand.—Choose—choose!"—"And how comes the key in your hand? and what is the condition of my liberation?" said Stanton.

.   .   .   .   .   .

The explanation occupied several pages, which, to the torture of young Melmoth, were wholly illegible. It seemed, however, to have been rejected by Stanton with the utmost rage and horror, for Melmoth at last made out,—"Begone, monster, demon!—begone to your native place. Even this mansion of horror trembles to contain you; its walls sweat, and its floors quiver, while you tread them."

.   .   .   .   .   .

The conclusion of this extraordinary manuscript was in such a state, that, in fifteen mouldy and crumbling pages, Melmoth could hardly make out that number of lines. No antiquarian, unfolding with trembling hand the calcined leaves of an Herculaneum manuscript, and hoping to discover some lost lines of the Aeneas in Virgil's own autograph, or at least some unutterable abomination of Petronius or Martial, happily elucidatory of the mysteries of the Spintriae, or the orgies of the Phallic worshipers, ever pored with more luckless diligence, or shook a head of more hopeless despondency over his task. He could but just make out what tended rather to excite than assuage that feverish thirst of curiosity which was consuming his inmost soul. The manuscript told no more of Melmoth, but mentioned that Stanton was finally liberated from his confinement,—that his pursuit of Melmoth was incessant and indefatigable,—that he himself allowed it to be a species of insanity,—that while he acknowledged it to be the master passion, he also felt it the master torment of his life. He again visited the Continent, returned to England,—pursued, inquired, traced, bribed, but in vain. The being whom he had met thrice, under circumstances so extraordinary, he was fated never to encounter again IN HIS LIFETIME. At length, discovering that he had been born in Ireland, he resolved to go there,—went, and found his pursuit again fruitless, and his inquiries unanswered. The family knew nothing of him, or at least what they knew or imagined, they prudently refused to disclose to a stranger, and Stanton departed unsatisfied. It is remarkable, that he too, as appeared from many half-obliterated pages of the manuscript, never disclosed to mortal the particulars of their conversation in the madhouse; and the slightest allusion to it threw him into fits of rage and gloom equally singular and alarming. He left the manuscript, however, in the hands of the family, possibly deeming, from their incuriosity, their apparent indifference to their relative, or their obvious unacquaintance with reading of any kind, manuscript or books, his deposit would be safe. He seems, in fact, to have acted like men, who, in distress at sea, intrust their letters and dispatches to a bottle sealed, and commit it to the waves. The last lines of the manuscript that were legible, were sufficiently extraordinary...

    .   .   .   .   .

"I have sought him everywhere.—The desire of meeting him once more is become as a burning fire within me,—it is the necessary condition of my existence. I have vainly sought him at last in Ireland, of which I find he is a native.— Perhaps our final meeting will be in...

    .   .   .   .   .

Such was the conclusion of the manuscript which Melmoth found in his uncle's closet. When he had finished it, he sunk down on the table near which he had been reading it, his face hid in his folded arms, his senses reeling, his mind in a mingled state of stupor and excitement. After a few moments, he raised himself with an involuntary start, and saw the picture gazing at him from its canvas. He was within ten inches of it as he sat, and the proximity appeared increased by the strong light that was accidentally thrown on it, and its being the only representation of a human figure in the room. Melmoth felt for a moment as if he were about to receive an explanation from its lips.

He gazed on it in return,—all was silent in the house,— they were alone together. The illusion subsided at length: and as the mind rapidly passes to opposite extremes, he remembered the injunction of his uncle to destroy the portrait. He seized it;—his hand shook at first, but the mouldering canvas appeared to assist him in the effort. He tore it from the frame with a cry half terrific, half triumphant,—it fell at his feet, and he shuddered as it fell. He expected to hear some fearful sounds, some unimaginable breathings of prophetic horror, follow this act of sacrilege, for such he felt it, to tear the portrait of his ancestor from his native walls. He paused and listened:—"There was no voice, nor any that answered;"—but as the wrinkled and torn canvas fell to the floor, its undulations gave the portrait the appearance of smiling. Melmoth felt horror indescribable at this transient and imaginary resuscitation of the figure. He caught it up, rushed into the next room, tore, cut, and hacked it in every direction, and eagerly watched the fragments that burned like tinder in the turf fire which had been lit in his room. As Melmoth saw the last blaze, he threw himself into bed, in hope of a deep and intense sleep. He had done what was required of him, and felt exhausted both in mind and body; but his slumber was not so sound as he had hoped for. The sullen light of the turf fire, burning but never blazing, disturbed him every moment. He turned and turned, but still there was the same red light glaring on, but not illuminating, the dusky furniture of the apartment. The wind was high that night, and as the creaking door swung on its hinges, every noise seemed like the sound of a hand struggling with the lock, or of a foot pausing on the threshold. But (for Melmoth never could decide) was it in a dream or not, that he saw the figure of his ancestor appear at the door?— hesitatingly as he saw him at first on the night of his uncle's death,—saw him enter the room, approach his bed, and heard him whisper, "You have burned me, then; but those are flames I can survive.—I am alive,—I am beside you." Melmoth started, sprung from his bed,—it was broad daylight. He looked round,—there was no human being in the room but himself. He felt a slight pain in the wrist of his right arm. He looked at it, it was black and blue, as from the recent gripe of a strong hand.

The Mysterious Mansion

By Honoré de Balzac

About a hundred yards from the town of Vendôme, on the borders of the Loire, there is an old gray house, surmounted by very high gables, and so completely isolated that neither tanyard nor shabby hostelry, such as you may find at the entrance to all small towns, exists in its immediate neighbourhood.

In front of this building, overlooking the river, is a garden, where the once well-trimmed box borders that used to define the walks now grow wild as they list. Several willows that spring from the Loire have grown as rapidly as the hedge that encloses it, and half conceal the house. The rich vegetation of those weeds that we call foul adorns the sloping shore. Fruit trees, neglected for the last ten years, no longer yield their harvest, and their shoots form coppices. The wall-fruit grows like hedges against the walls. Paths once gravelled are overgrown with moss, but, to tell the truth, there is no trace of a path. From the height of the hill, to which cling the ruins of the old castle of the Dukes of Vendôme, the only spot whence the eye can plunge into this enclosure, it strikes you that, at a time not easy to determine, this plot of land was the delight of a country gentleman, who cultivated roses and tulips and horticulture in general, and who was besides a lover of fine fruit. An arbour is still visible, or rather the débris of an arbour, where there is a table that time has not quite destroyed. The aspect of this garden of bygone days suggests the negative joys of peaceful, provincial life, as one might reconstruct the life of a worthy tradesman by reading the epitaph on his tombstone. As if to complete the sweetness and sadness of the ideas that possess one's soul, one of the walls displays a sun-dial decorated with the following commonplace Christian inscription: "Ultimam cogita!" The roof of this house is horribly dilapidated, the shutters are always closed, the balconies are covered with swallows' nests, the doors are perpetually shut, weeds have drawn green lines in the cracks of the flights of steps, the locks and bolts are rusty. Sun, moon, winter, summer, and snow have worn the panelling, warped the boards, gnawed the paint. The lugubrious silence which reigns there is only broken by birds, cats, martins, rats and mice, free to course to and fro, to fight and to eat each other. Everywhere an invisible hand has graven the word mystery.

Should your curiosity lead you to glance at this house from the side that points to the road, you would perceive a great door which the children of the place have riddled with holes. I afterward heard that this door had been closed for the last ten years. Through the holes broken by the boys you would have observed the perfect harmony that existed between the façades of both garden and courtyard. In both the same disorder prevails. Tufts of weed encircle the paving-stones. Enormous cracks furrow the walls, round whose blackened crests twine the thousand garlands of the pellitory. The steps are out of joint, the wire of the bell is rusted, the spouts are cracked. What fire from heaven has fallen here? What tribunal has decreed that salt should be strewn on this dwelling? Has God been blasphemed, has France been here betrayed? These are the questions we ask ourselves, but get no answer from the crawling things that haunt the place. The empty and deserted house is a gigantic enigma, of which the key is lost. In bygone times it was a small fief, and bears the name of the Grande Bretèche.

I inferred that I was not the only person to whom my good landlady had communicated the secret of which I was to be the sole recipient, and I prepared to listen.

"Sir," she said, "when the Emperor sent the Spanish prisoners of war and others here, the Government quartered on me a young Spaniard who had been sent to Vendôme on parole. Parole notwithstanding he went out every day to show himself to the sous-préfet. He was a Spanish grandee! Nothing less! His name ended in os and dia, something like Burgos de Férédia. I have his name on my books; you can read it if you like. Oh! but he was a handsome young man for a Spaniard; they are all said to be ugly. He was only five feet and a few inches high, but he was well-grown; he had small hands that he took such care of; ah! you should have seen! He had as many brushes for his hands as a woman for her whole dressing apparatus! He had thick black hair, a fiery eye, his skin was rather bronzed, but I liked the look of it. He wore the finest linen I have ever seen on any one, although I have had princesses staying here, and, among others, General Bertrand, the Duke and Duchess d'Abrantés, Monsieur Decazes, and the King of Spain. He didn't eat much; but his manners were so polite, so amiable, that one could not owe him a grudge. Oh! I was very fond of him, although he didn't open his lips four times in the day, and it was impossible to keep up a conversation with him. For if you spoke to him, he did not answer. It was a fad, a mania with them all, I heard say. He read his breviary like a priest, he went to Mass and to all the services regularly. Where did he sit? Two steps from the chapel of Madame de Merret. As he took his place there the first time he went to church, nobody suspected him of any intention in so doing. Besides, he never raised his eyes from his prayer-book, poor young man!

After that, sir, in the evening he would walk on the mountains, among the castle ruins. It was the poor man's only amusement, it reminded him of his country. They say that Spain is all mountains! From the commencement of his imprisonment he stayed out late. I was anxious when I found that he did not come home before midnight; but we got accustomed to this fancy of his. He took the key of the door, and we left off sitting up for him. He lodged in a house of ours in the Rue des Casernes. After that, one of our stable-men told us that in the evening when he led the horses to the water, he thought he had seen the Spanish grandee swimming far down the river like a live fish. When he returned, I told him to take care of the rushes; he appeared vexed to have been seen in the water. At last, one day, or rather one morning, we did not find him in his room; he had not returned. After searching everywhere, I found some writing in the drawer of a table, where there were fifty gold pieces of Spain that are called doubloons and were worth about five thousand francs; and ten thousand francs' worth of diamonds in a small sealed box. The writing said, that in case he did not return, he left us the money and the diamonds, on condition of paying for Masses to thank God for his escape, and for his salvation. In those days my husband had not been taken from me; he hastened to seek him everywhere.

"And now for the strange part of the story. He brought home the Spaniard's clothes, that he had discovered under a big stone, in a sort of pilework by the river-side near the castle, nearly opposite to the Grande Bretêche. My husband had gone there so early that no one had seen him. After reading the letter, he burned the clothes, and according to Count Fédéria's desire we declared that he had escaped. The sous-préfet sent all the gendarmerie in pursuit of him; but brust! they never caught him. Lepas believed that the Spaniard had drowned himself. I, sir, don't think so; I am more inclined to believe that he had something to do with the affair of Madame de Merret, seeing that Rosalie told me that the crucifix, that her mistress thought so much of, that she had it buried with her, was of ebony and silver. Now in the beginning of his stay here, Monsieur de Fédéria had one in ebony and silver, that I never saw him with later. Now, sir, don't you consider that I need have no scruples about the Spaniard's fifteen thousand francs, and that I have a right to them?"

"Certainly; but you haven't tried to question Rosalie?" I said.

"Oh, yes, indeed, sir; but to no purpose! the girl's like a wall. She knows something, but it is impossible to get her to talk."

After exchanging a few more words with me, my landlady left me a prey to vague and gloomy thoughts, to a romantic curiosity, and a religious terror not unlike the profound impression produced on us when by night, on entering a dark church, we perceive a faint light under high arches; a vague figure glides by—the rustle of a robe or cassock is heard, and we shudder.

Suddenly the Grande Bretêche and its tall weeds, its barred windows, its rusty ironwork, its closed doors, its deserted apartments, appeared like a fantastic apparition before me. I essayed to penetrate the mysterious dwelling, and to find the knot of its dark story—the drama that had killed three persons. In my eyes Rosalie became the most interesting person in Vendôme. As I studied her, I discovered the traces of secret care, despite the radiant health that shone in her plump countenance. There was in her the germ of remorse or hope; her attitude revealed a secret, like the attitude of a bigot who prays to excess, or of the infanticide who ever hears the last cry of her child. Yet her manners were rough and ingenuous—her silly smile was not that of a criminal, and could you but have seen the great kerchief that encompassed her portly bust, framed and laced in by a lilac and blue cotton gown, you would have dubbed her innocent. No, I thought, I will not leave Vendôme without learning the history of the Grande Bretêche. To gain my ends I will strike up a friendship with Rosalie, if needs be. "Rosalie," said I, one evening.

"Sir?"

"You are not married?"

She started slightly.

"Oh, I can find plenty of men, when the fancy takes me to be made miserable," she said, laughing.

She soon recovered from the effects of her emotion, for all women, from the great lady to the maid of the inn, possess a composure that is peculiar to them.

"You are too good-looking and well favoured to be short of lovers. But tell me, Rosalie, why did you take service in an inn after leaving Madame de Merret? Did she leave you nothing to live on?"

"Oh, yes! But, sir, my place is the best in all Vendôme." The reply was one of those that judges and lawyers would call evasive. Rosalie appeared to me to be situated in this romantic history like the square in the midst of a chessboard. She was at the heart of the truth and chief interest; she seemed to me to be bound in the very knot of it. The conquest of Rosalie was no longer to be an ordinary siege—in this girl was centred the last chapter of a novel, therefore from this moment Rosalie became the object of my preference.

One morning I said to Rosalie: "Tell me all you know about Madame de Merret."

"Oh!" she replied in terror, "do not ask that of me, Monsieur Horace."
Her pretty face fell—her clear, bright colour faded—and her eyes lost their innocent brightness.

"Well, then," she said, at last, "if you must have it so, I will tell you about it; but promise to keep my secret!"

"Done! my dear girl, I must keep your secret with the honour of a thief, which is the most loyal in the world."

Were I to transcribe Rosalie's diffuse eloquence faithfully, an entire volume would scarcely contain it; so I shall abridge.

The room occupied by Madame de Merret at the Bretêche was on the ground floor. A little closet about four feet deep, built in the thickness of the wall, served as her wardrobe. Three months before the eventful evening of which I am about to speak, Madame de Merret had been so seriously indisposed that her husband had left her to herself in her own apartment, while he occupied another on the first floor. By one of those chances that it is impossible to foresee, he returned home from the club (where he was accustomed to read the papers and discuss politics with the inhabitants of the place) two hours later than usual. His wife supposed him to be at home, in bed and asleep. But the invasion of France had been the subject of a most animated discussion; the billiard-match had been exciting, he had lost forty francs, an enormous sum for Vendôme, where every one hoards, and where manners are restricted within the limits of a praiseworthy modesty, which perhaps is the source of the true happiness that no Parisian covets. For some time past Monsieur de Merret had been satisfied to ask Rosalie if his wife had gone to bed; and on her reply, which was always in the affirmative, had immediately gained his own room with the good temper engendered by habit and confidence. On entering his house, he took it into his head to go and tell his wife of his misadventure, perhaps by way of consolation. At dinner he found Madame de Merret most coquettishly attired. On his way to the club it had occurred to him that his wife was restored to health, and that her convalescence had added to her beauty. He was, as husbands are wont to be, somewhat slow in making this discovery. Instead of calling Rosalie, who was occupied just then in watching the cook and coachman play a difficult hand at brisque, Monsieur de Merret went to his wife's room by the light of a lantern that he deposited on the first step of the staircase. His unmistakable step resounded under the vaulted corridor. At the moment that the Count turned the handle of his wife's door, he fancied he could hear the door of the closet I spoke of close; but when he entered Madame de Merret was alone before the fireplace. The husband thought ingenuously that Rosalie was in the closet, yet a suspicion that jangled in his ear put him on his guard. He looked at his wife and saw in her eyes I know not what wild and hunted expression.

"You are very late," she said. Her habitually pure, sweet voice seemed changed to him. Monsieur de Merret did not reply, for at that moment Rosalie entered. It was a thunderbolt for him. He strode about the room, passing from one window to the other, with mechanical motion and folded arms.

"Have you heard bad news, or are you unwell?" inquired his wife timidly, while Rosalie undressed her.

He kept silent.

"You can leave me," said Madame de Merret to her maid; "I will put my hair in curl papers myself."

From the expression of her husband's face she foresaw trouble, and wished to be alone with him. When Rosalie had gone, or was supposed to have gone (for she stayed in the corridor for a few minutes), Monsieur de Merret came and stood in front of his wife, and said coldly to her:

"Madame, there is someone in your closet!" She looked calmly at her husband and replied simply:

"No, sir."

This answer was heartrending to Monsieur de Merret; he did not believe in it. Yet his wife had never appeared to him purer or more saintly than at that moment. He rose to open the closet door; Madame de Merret took his hand, looked at him with an expression of melancholy, and said in a voice that betrayed singular emotion:

"If you find no one there, remember this, all will be over between us!" The extraordinary dignity of his wife's manner restored the Count's profound esteem for her, and inspired him with one of those resolutions that only lack a vaster stage to become immortal.

"No," said he, "Josephine, I will not go there. In either case it would separate us forever. Hear me, I know how pure you are at heart, and that your life is a holy one. You would not commit a mortal sin to save your life."

At these words Madame de Merret turned a haggard gaze upon her husband.

"Here, take your crucifix," he added. "Swear to me before God that there is no one in there; I will believe you, I will never open that door."

Madame de Merret took the crucifix and said:

"I swear."

"Louder," said the husband, "and repeat 'I swear before God that there is no one in that closet'."

She repeated the sentence calmly.

"That will do," said Monsieur de Merret, coldly.

After a moment of silence:

"I never saw this pretty toy before," he said, examining the ebony crucifix inlaid with silver, and most artistically chiselled.

"I found it at Duvivier's, who bought it of a Spanish monk when the prisoners passed through Vendôme last year."

"Ah!" said Monsieur de Merret, as he replaced the crucifix on the nail, and he rang. Rosalie did not keep him waiting. Monsieur de Merret went quickly to meet her, led her to the bay window that opened on to the garden and whispered to her:
"Listen! I know that Gorenflot wishes to marry you, poverty is the only drawback, and you told him that you would be his wife if he found the means to establish himself as a master mason. Well! go and fetch him, tell him to come here with his trowel and tools. Manage not to awaken any one in his house but himself; his fortune will be more than your desires. Above all, leave this room without babbling, otherwise—" He frowned. Rosalie went away, he recalled her.

"Here, take my latchkey," he said. "Jean!" then cried Monsieur de Merret, in tones of thunder in the corridor. Jean, who was at the same time his coachman and his confidential servant, left his game of cards and came.

HONORÉ DE BALZAC

"Go to bed, all of you," said his master, signing to him to approach; and the Count added, under his breath: "When they are all asleep—asleep, d'ye hear?—you will come down and tell me." Monsieur de Merret, who had not lost sight of his wife all the time he was giving his orders, returned quietly to her at the fireside and began to tell her of the game of billiards and the talk of the club. When Rosalie returned she found Monsieur and Madame de Merret conversing very amicably.

The Count had lately had all the ceilings of his reception rooms on the ground floor repaired. Plaster of Paris is difficult to obtain in Vendôme; the carriage raises its price. The Count had therefore bought a good deal, being well aware that he could find plenty of purchasers for whatever might remain over. This circumstance inspired him with the design he was about to execute.

"Sir, Gorenflot has arrived," said Rosalie in low tones.

"Show him in," replied the Count in loud tones.

Madame de Merret turned rather pale when she saw the mason.

"Gorenflot," said her husband, "go and fetch bricks from the coachhouse, and bring sufficient to wall up the door of this closet; you will use the plaster I have over to coat the wall with." Then calling Rosalie and the workman aside:

"Listen, Gorenflot," he said in an undertone, "you will sleep here to-night. But to-morrow you will have a passport to a foreign country, to a town to which I will direct you. I shall give you six thousand francs for your journey. You will stay ten years in that town; if you do not like it, you may establish yourself in another, provided it be in the same country. You will pass through Paris, where you will await me. There I will insure you an additional six thousand francs by contract, which will be paid to you on your return, provided you have fulfilled the conditions of our bargain. This is the price for your absolute silence as to what you are about to do to-night. As to you, Rosalie, I will give you ten thousand francs on the day of your wedding, on condition of

65

your marrying Gorenflot; but if you wish to marry, you must hold your tongues; or—no dowry."

"Rosalie," said Madame de Merret, "do my hair."

The husband walked calmly up and down, watching the door, the mason, and his wife, but without betraying any insulting doubts. Madame de Merret chose a moment when the workman was unloading bricks and her husband was at the other end of the room to say to Rosalie: "A thousand francs a year for you, my child, if you can tell Gorenflot to leave a chink at the bottom." Then out loud, she added coolly:

"Go and help him!"

Monsieur and Madame de Merret were silent all the time that Gorenflot took to brick up the door. This silence, on the part of the husband, who did not choose to furnish his wife with a pretext for saying things of a double meaning, had its purpose; on the part of Madame de Merret it was either pride or prudence. When the wall was about half-way up, the sly workman took advantage of a moment when the Count's back was turned, to strike a blow with his trowel in one of the glass panes of the closet-door. This act informed Madame de Merret that Rosalie had spoken to Gorenflot.

All three then saw a man's face; it was dark and gloomy with black hair and eyes of flame. Before her husband turned, the poor woman had time to make a sign to the stranger that signified: Hope!

At four o'clock, toward dawn, for it was the month of September, the construction was finished. The mason was handed over to the care of Jean, and Monsieur de Merret went to bed in his wife's room.

On rising the following morning, he said carelessly:

"The deuce! I must go to the Mairie for the passport." He put his hat on his head, advanced three steps toward the door, altered his mind and took the crucifix.

His wife trembled for joy. "He is going to Duvivier," she thought. As soon as the Count had left, Madame de Merret rang for Rosalie; then in a terrible voice:

"The trowel, the trowel!" she cried, "and quick to work! I saw how Gorenflot did it; we shall have time to make a hole and to mend it again."

In the twinkling of an eye, Rosalie brought a sort of mattock to her mistress, who with unparalleled ardour set about demolishing the wall. She had already knocked out several bricks and was preparing to strike a more decisive blow when she perceived Monsieur de Merret behind her. She fainted.

"Lay Madame on her bed," said the Count coldly. He had foreseen what would happen in his absence and had set a trap for his wife; he had simply written to the mayor, and had sent for Duvivier. The jeweller arrived just as the room had been put in order.

"Duvivier," inquired the Count, "did you buy crucifixes of the Spaniards who passed through here?"

"No, sir."

"That will do, thank you," he said, looking at his wife like a tiger. "Jean," he added, "you will see that my meals are served in the Countess's room; she is ill, and I shall not leave her until she has recovered."

The cruel gentleman stayed with his wife for twenty days. In the beginning, when there were sounds in the walled closet, and Josephine attempted to implore his pity for the dying stranger, he replied, without permitting her to say a word:

"You have sworn on the cross that there is no one there."

The Flayed Hand

By Guy De Maupassant

One evening about eight months ago I met with some college comrades at the lodgings of our friend Louis R. We drank punch and smoked, talked of literature and art, and made jokes like any other company of young men. Suddenly the door flew open, and one who had been my friend since boyhood burst in like a hurricane.

"Guess where I come from?" he cried.

"I bet on the Mabille," responded one. "No," said another, "you are too gay; you come from borrowing money, from burying a rich uncle, or from pawning your watch." "You are getting sober," cried a third, "and, as you scented the punch in Louis' room, you came up here to get drunk again."

"You are all wrong," he replied. "I come from P., in Normandy, where I have spent eight days, and whence I have brought one of my friends, a great criminal, whom I ask permission to present to you."

With these words he drew from his pocket a long, black hand, from which the skin had been stripped. It had been severed at the wrist. Its dry and shrivelled shape, and the narrow, yellowed nails still clinging to the fingers, made it frightful to look upon. The muscles, which showed that Its first owner had been possessed of great strength, were bound in place by a strip of parchment-like skin.

"Just fancy," said my friend, "the other day they sold the effects of an old sorcerer, recently deceased, well known in all the country. Every Saturday night he used to go to witch gatherings on a broomstick; he practised the white magic and the black, gave blue milk to the cows, and made them wear tails like that of the companion of Saint Anthony. The old scoundrel always had a deep affection for this hand, which, he said, was that of a celebrated criminal, executed in 1736 for having thrown his lawful wife head first into a well—for which I do not blame him—and then hanging in the belfry the priest who had married him. After this double exploit he went away, and, during his subsequent career, which was brief but exciting, he robbed twelve travellers, smoked a score of monks in their monastery, and made a seraglio of a convent."

"But what are you going to do with this horror?" we cried.

"Eh! parbleu! I will make it the handle to my door-bell and frighten my creditors."

"My friend," said Henry Smith, a big, phlegmatic Englishman, "I believe that this hand is only a kind of Indian meat, preserved by a new process; I advise you to make bouillon of it."

"Rail not, messieurs," said, with the utmost sang froid, a medical student who was three-quarters drunk, "but if you follow my advice, Pierre, you will give this piece of human debris Christian burial, for fear lest its owner should come to demand it. Then, too, this hand has acquired some bad habits, for you know the proverb, 'Who has killed will kill.'"

"And who has drank will drink," replied the host as he poured out a big glass of punch for the student, who emptied it at a draught and slid dead drunk under the table. His sudden dropping out of the company was greeted with a burst of laughter, and Pierre, raising his glass and saluting the hand, cried:

"I drink to the next visit of thy master."

Then the conversation turned upon other subjects, and shortly afterward each returned to his lodgings. About two o'clock the next day, as I was passing Pierre's door, I entered and found him reading and smoking.

"Well, how goes it?" said I. "Very well," he responded. "And your hand?" "My hand? Did you not see it on the bell-pull? I put it there when I returned home last night. But, apropos of this, what do you think? Some idiot, doubtless to play a stupid joke on me, came ringing at my door towards midnight. I demanded who was there, but as no one replied, I went back to bed again, and to sleep."

At this moment the door opened and the landlord, a fat and extremely impertinent person, entered without saluting us.

"Sir," said he, "I pray you to take away immediately that carrion which you have hung to your bell-pull. Unless you do this I shall be compelled to ask you to leave."

"Sir," responded Pierre, with much gravity, "you insult a hand which does not merit it. Know you that it belonged to a man of high breeding?"

The landlord turned on his heel and made his exit, without speaking. Pierre followed him, detached the hand and affixed it to the bell-cord hanging in his alcove.

70

"That is better," he said. "This hand, like the 'Brother, all must die,' of the Trappists, will give my thoughts a serious turn every night before I sleep."

At the end of an hour I left him and returned to my own apartment.

I slept badly the following night, was nervous and agitated, and several times awoke with a start. Once I imagined, even, that a man had broken into my room, and I sprang up and searched the closets and under the bed. Towards six o'clock in the morning I was commencing to doze at last, when a loud knocking at my door made me jump from my couch. It was my friend Pierre's servant, half dressed, pale and trembling.

"Ah, sir!" cried he, sobbing, "my poor master. Someone has murdered him."

I dressed myself hastily and ran to Pierre's lodgings. The house was full of people disputing together, and everything was in a commotion. Everyone was talking at the same time, recounting and commenting on the occurrence in all sorts of ways. With great difficulty I reached the bed-room, made myself known to those guarding the door and was permitted to enter. Four agents of police were standing in the middle of the apartment, pencils in hand, examining every detail, conferring in low voices and writing from time to time in their note-books. Two doctors were in consultation by the bed on which lay the unconscious form of Pierre. He was not dead, but his face was fixed in an expression of the most awful terror. His eyes were open their widest, and the dilated pupils seemed to regard fixedly, with unspeakable horror, something unknown and frightful. His hands were clinched. I raised the quilt, which covered his body from the chin downward, and saw on his neck, deeply sunk in the flesh, the marks of fingers. Some drops of blood spotted his shirt. At that moment one thing struck me. I chanced to notice that the shrivelled hand was no longer attached to the bell-cord. The doctors had doubtless removed it to avoid the comments of those entering the chamber where the wounded man lay, because the appearance of this hand was indeed frightful. I did not inquire what had become of it.

I now clip from a newspaper of the next day the story of the crime with all the details that the police were able to procure:

"A frightful attempt was made yesterday on the life of young M. Pierre B., student, who belongs to one of the best families in Normandy. He returned home about ten o'clock in the evening, and excused his valet, Bouvin, from further attendance upon him, saying that he felt fatigued and was going to bed. Towards midnight Bouvin was suddenly awakened by the furious ringing of his master's bell. He was afraid, and lighted a lamp and waited. The bell was silent about a minute, then rang again with such vehemence that the domestic, mad with fright, flew from his room to awaken the concierge, who ran to summon the police, and, at the end of about fifteen minutes, two policemen forced open the door. A horrible sight met their eyes. The furniture was overturned, giving evidence of a fearful struggle between the victim and his assailant. In the middle of the room, upon his back, his body rigid, with livid face and frightfully dilated eyes, lay, motionless, young Pierre B., bearing upon his neck the deep imprints of five fingers. Dr. Bourdean was called immediately, and his report says that the aggressor must have been possessed of prodigious strength and have had an extraordinarily thin and sinewy hand, because the fingers left in the flesh of the victim five holes like those from a pistol ball, and had penetrated until they almost met. There is no clue to the motive of the crime or to its perpetrator. The police are making a thorough investigation."

The following appeared in the same newspaper next day:

"M. Pierre B., the victim of the frightful assault of which we published an account yesterday, has regained consciousness after two hours of the most assiduous care by Dr. Bourdean. His life is not in danger, but it is strongly feared that he has lost his reason. No trace has been found of his assailant."

My poor friend was indeed insane. For seven months I visited him daily at the hospital where we had placed him, but he did not recover the light of reason. In his delirium strange words escaped him, and, like all madmen, he had one fixed idea: he believed himself continually pursued by a spectre. One day they came for me in haste, saying he was worse, and when I arrived I found him dying. For two hours he remained very calm, then, suddenly, rising from his bed in spite of our efforts, he cried, waving his arms as if a prey to the most awful terror: "Take it away! Take it away! It strangles me! Help! Help!" Twice he made the circuit of the room, uttering horrible screams, then fell face downward, dead.

As he was an orphan I was charged to take his body to the little village of P., in Normandy, where his parents were buried. It was the place from which he had arrived the evening he found us drinking punch in Louis R.'s room, when he had presented to us the flayed hand. His body was inclosed in a leaden coffin, and four days afterwards I walked sadly beside the old curé, who had given him his first lessons, to the little cemetery where they dug his grave. It was a beautiful day, and sunshine from a cloudless sky flooded the earth. Birds sang from the blackberry bushes where many a time when we were children we had stolen to eat the fruit.

Again I saw Pierre and myself creeping along behind the hedge and slipping through the gap that we knew so well, down at the end of the little plot where they bury the poor. Again we would return to the house with cheeks and lips black with the juice of the berries we had eaten. I looked at the bushes; they were covered with fruit; mechanically I picked some and bore it to my mouth. The curé had opened his breviary, and was muttering his prayers in a low voice. I heard at the end of the walk the spades of the grave-diggers who were opening the tomb. Suddenly they called out, the curé closed his book, and we went to see what they wished of us. They had found a coffin; in digging a stroke of the pickaxe had started the cover, and we perceived within a skeleton of unusual stature, lying on its back, its hollow eyes seeming yet to menace and defy us. I was troubled, I know not why, and almost afraid.

"Hold!" cried one of the men, "look there! One of the rascal's hands has been severed at the wrist. Ah, here it is!" and he picked up from beside the body a huge withered hand, and held it out to us. "See," cried the other, laughing, "see how he glares at you, as if he would spring at your throat to make you give him back his hand."

"Go," said the curé, "leave the dead in peace, and close the coffin. We will make poor Pierre's grave elsewhere."

The next day all was finished, and I returned to Paris, after having left fifty francs with the old curé for masses to be said for the repose of the soul of him whose sepulchre we had troubled.

The Ruins of the Abbey of Fitz-Martin

by Anonymous

The Abbey of Fitz-Martin had been once famous for its riches and grandeur, and, as a monastery, was dedicated to St Catherine; but the subsequent irregularity of its order, together with the despotic tyranny of one of its ancient lords, had stripped it by slow but sure degrees of all its former wealth and consequence; insomuch, that the haughty Baron had, under unjust pretences, demanded heavy contributions, to assist in carrying on the war between the first Edward and the nearly subdued Scots. His only excuse for such an open violation of ecclesiastic rights was grounded on a discovery he pretended he had made, of one of the nuns having broken the sacred rules of her profession, by a disregard to her vows of vestal celibacy. The haughty Baron seized greedily this circumstance, as the means of succeeding in his ambitious designs, and determined to humble the pride and insolence of the superiors, since the land belonged originally to his ancestors, and was transmitted to himself with powers to exact homage and fee from the heads of the monastery for this only part of their dependence on laical jurisdiction. For this latter purpose, the Baron, as Lord Patron of the holy community, entered the abbey, and demanded from the superiors not only a large subsidy of money, but an acknowledgement of their obedience; and, to cover his injustice, pretended it was designed for the further prosecution of the Holy Wars.

The superiors proudly refused compliance, and, in angry tones, threatened an appeal to Rome, with a dreadful anathema on the head of the daring violator, if he persisted in his presumptions.

But the Baron knew the surety of his proceedings, and, with a smile of malicious triumph, exposed his knowledge of the crimes of Sister St Anna, even relating at full his acquaintance with the proof of her lapse from that sacred vow, which for ever enjoined the community of a monastery to celibacy. The fathers of the order, when summoned to the council, heard the account with confusion and dismay, and entreated time to search into the truth of the Baron's assertions. The crafty Baron knew the advantage he had over them; and, to increase their fears of the dreaded exposure, quitted the abbey, in haughty and forbidding silence, without deigning to answer their petitions.

The unhappy community of the once proud monastery of St Catherine, at length, harassed by their dread of an exposure, and the total loss of all their wealth, by multiplied and never ceasing demands, became dependant on its tyrannic Baron, who kept the monks in such entire and arbitrary subjection, that in the course of a very few years, the abbey became nearly quite forsaken by its once imperious masters; when, at length, the Baron having disclosed to the King the dissolute manners of the order, and supplying Edward also with a large sum of money, that Monarch unknowingly rewarded his treachery with the hereditary possession of the abbey, and all its tenures, revenues and riches.

The Baron, therefore, took undisputed possession of his new acquisition, which he soon transformed into a princely habitation. But tradition says, that its imperious master did not, though surrounded by the possession of a mine of wealth, enjoy that expected ease, and inward happiness, which the gratification of his lawless wishes led him to hope for. For he is reported ever after to have been subject to gloomy passions, and melancholy abstractions of mind, which often ended in vehement paroxisms of madness. An imperfectly handed tradition still existed, which related, that the spectre of St Anna, the unhappy instrument of his destruction to the monastery, had repeatedly appeared to the Baron, to warn him of his heinous offences, and even accuse him as the cause of her ruin, and subsequent punishment by death. Certain it is, that various reports and conjectures had arisen in the minds of the ignorant; some tending to involve the Baron in the guilt of being the unknown seducer of Anna, for the purpose of completing his avaricious designs. But the real truth of her destiny was totally involved in silence; as, soon after the Baron had exposed to the superiors his knowledge of her dereliction, she had suddenly disappeared from the community, nor was ever heard of after. Whatever was in reality her dreadful end is still unknown. But the Baron lived not long to enjoy the splendour of his ill-gained riches. He was heard to confess, that peace of mind was for ever banished from his heart; and, though lying on the downy couches of luxury, yet did he never after enjoy a calm undisturbed conscience. His death was the departure of guilty horror, and alarm for the future; and he quitted the world with curses and execrations on himself, leaving no child to inherit the abbey, which descended to his next heir; who, being every way unlike his uncle, refused to reside in a place that had been obtained by fraud and injustice. From this period the abbey, for near a century and a half, had acknowledged several lords, but was seldom honoured, for any length of time, by the presence of its possessors, who were in general eager to shun a place, whose traditional history teemed with dark and mysterious records. The owners of the abbey were too superiorly gifted with Fortune's treasures, and the spectred traditions of St Anna kept them from ever approaching its decayed towers. Its lands, therefore, remaining untilled, soon added increase to the surrounding forests, and were suffered to become useless, and over-run with the luxuriance of uncultivated nature.

The last owner deceased, was a distant relation of the present inheritor, Sir Thomas Fitz-Martin, who was driven by severe misfortune, and the loss of a most amiable wife, to seek its long-deserted ruins, to hide himself and family from the dreadful consequences of an over-ruling fate which no human wisdom could avert, but in the hoped-for security of this long-forgotten retreat.

Yet the suddenness of his journey, its long and fatiguing continuance, together with the gloomy, remote, and even terrific habitation he was speedily approaching, began to raise fears and doubts in the minds of the domestics, who shrunk back, declaring it impossible to venture into so terrific and ruinous a place. Sir Thomas had never but once seen it, and that many years since, and even shuddered as he again reviewed its dreary and frowning exterior, and half wished that his haste had not led him to choose so desolate a place for his future abode. At that moment the carriage suddenly stopping, at some little distance from an open avenue that led immediately to the abbey, Owen demanded if he was to proceed further, or if his Honour had not better turn into another path, and seek the nearest way out of the dismal forest; 'for surely, my Lord will never think of entering yon frightful old ruin, which, I dare say, will fall, and crush us alive beneath its humble battlements: or perhaps we shall have to encounter a battle with an army of ghosts and hobgoblins, who will dispute our right of admission within their tottering territories.'

'Peace, I command you,' exclaimed Sir Thomas. 'I thought you, at least, possessed more courage, than to admit the impression of such idle fears as even your female companions would blush to express. The seat of my ancestors, though long deserted and now perhaps destitute of every comfort, has, I will vouch for it, nothing that can justly alarm or excite cowardice in the minds of my servants. If, however, yourself, or any of your companions, fear to enter with your lord the building he has chosen for his future abode, they have free permission to remain with the carriage till day-light, whilst I and my daughter will alone seek our admission within a mansion that hereafter shall become our chief residence.'

Sir Thomas, at length descending from the vehicle, walked, with cautious inspection, a considerable way beneath the walls, before he arrived at the heavy gates of entrance. They were, however, securely closed, and resisted his attempts to force them, with an obstinacy that surprised him. Calling loudly to his terror-stricken people, he commanded them, on their approach, to join their efforts with his; but the gates proved the strength of their interior holds, and none of the fastenings yielded to their attacks. Tired with this fruitless labour, yet wondering at the security with which they were barricaded, Sir Thomas paused once more, and in that interval the idea flashed on his mind, that the abbey might possibly be inhabited; though well he knew he had given no one permission to enter its precincts; and the traditional terrors of the place he thought were a sufficient guard against all unknown intruders. Yet it was not unlikely, that if it were indeed inhabited, it was become the dreadful haunt of banditti, to whom the lonely situation of the forest rendered it a very favourable concealment for the practice of their daring profession. For a moment this fearful supposition rendered Sir Thomas undecided, and he remained irresolute how to proceed, from the dread of exposing his family to more real dangers than the imaginary ones of Owen, till a violent flash of lightning ended his doubts; as it glanced in an instant on the walls of the abbey, and displayed its tottering turrets and broken casements. It shewed also, at no great distance, a small postern, whose weak state seemed to promise greater success; and they determined to try it if they could not here find a more willing admission. The postern was extremely old, and seemed only held by the bolt of the lock, which soon gave way to the attack of the travellers; and crossing beneath a heavy Gothic arch, they found themselves within the area of the first court. Sir Thomas, followed by his trembling attendants, was hastening forward, till recollecting the females in the carriage were left unguarded, he ordered one of the men to return instantly, and await with them the event of their lord's bold adventure to gain shelter within the ruin. Owen summoned up a sort of desperate courage, and declared his intention of attending his master: and lighting a torch, he followed his calm and undaunted conductor, who now advanced with caution through the wide area of a second court, which, being covered with crumbling fragments of the ruins, rendered his advances difficult, and even dangerous. At length he reached a flight of steps, that seemed to lead to the grand portal of entrance. Sir Thomas, however, determined to ascend; and Owen, though tottering beneath his own weight with terrors, dared not interpose his resistance: his trembling hand held the light to the great folding doors, and Sir Thomas, after some efforts, burst them open, and entered what appeared an immense hall, terminating in vistas of huge pillars, whose lofty heads, like the roof they supported, were impervious to the faint rays of the torch, and enveloped in an awful and misty gloom, beyond expression impressive and solemn, and creating astonishing sensations in the startled beholder.

At length Sir Thomas's progress was stopped by some steps, that led up to a Gothic door, which, with no little difficulty, he forced back, and entering its dark precincts, found himself within a large antique room, with the forms of several crumbling pieces of furniture, which, from the number of its raised couches, now covered with blackness, seemed evidently the remnants of a chamber that had once been stately and magnificent. Sir Thomas examined it well. The walls, though dripping with damp, seemed tolerably entire, and to promise security from the dangers of the night; and as he had as yet seen nothing to excite alarm or dread, he hastened to the carriage, and declared to its inmates his resolution. The females knowing that, as they had proceeded thus far, to retract from their fearful enterprise was now become impracticable, obeyed with trembling and reluctant steps, and, supported by their male companions, slowly advanced; whilst Sir Thomas, taking Rosaline in his arms, conveyed her to the abbey.

Owen and Rowland, who had, by the command of their master, cut down several branches from the forest, now set them alight within the wide spreading hearth, whose brisk and crackling blaze soon dispelled the damp and glooms of a dreary chamber, and at length compelled even the long-stretched countenances of the females to relax into something like a smile; and the remembered fatigue and danger of their perilous journey through the forest, when compared with their present shelter, and the comforts of a welcome and plentiful meal, succeeded at last in making a very visible alteration. The repast being ended, Sir Thomas commanded Owen to place before the fire some of the strongest couches he could find, and cover them with packages, and compose themselves to rest. The servants, who had dreaded the thoughts of being obliged to pass the night in the chamber, were grateful for this considerate permission; and reclining themselves on the couches, they soon forgot the terrors and dangers they had felt, and became alike insensible to their forlorn situation, and to the storm which howled without, and now shook the trembling fabric, with each fresh gust of wind that assailed its ruined towers.

Sir Thomas was the first of the slumbering travellers that awoke. Convinced that it was day, from a ray of light that shone through a broken window shutter, he hastened to arise; for, since he was assured he should sleep no more, he resolved not to disturb his wearied domestics, but use the present interval to search the abbey. He proceeded to a large folding door on the west side, which he concluded must have been the grand entrance; but he declined, for the present, any further examination of the outside of the building; and turning to the left, advanced to a folding door, deeply fixed within a Gothic portal, which opening harshly to his efforts, let him, with astonishment, into a long suite of rooms, which, notwithstanding their silent, deserted, ruinous state, he was rejoiced to find might again be rendered habitable, and in a little time even convenient and comfortable.

They were eight in number, and still retained many remnants of furniture, which, though covered with mildew and dust, and crumbling to tatters, evidently witnessed the splendour of its former owner. He was satisfied that these chambers would amply answer his present wants, and rejoiced to find them in such a state as to make their repair not only possible but easy.

Proceeding forward through this vast extent of chambers, Sir Thomas felt that every former surmise of robbers was at an end, as he had as yet met with not a single circumstance that could in any degree confirm it. He was now hastening back to his family, who, should they have awoke, might experience no inconsiderable alarm.

Having descended for this purpose, he found himself, as he turned on the left, in a long but narrow gallery or passage; passing forward, he opened with much labour several old doors, in hopes they would bring him into a passage leading into the great hall or church; but they only presented a number of weak and dangerous recesses, perhaps formerly cells of the monastery, whose flooring was so much decayed, and in some places fallen in, as to render further progress impossible. Quitting the fruitless search, he proceeded to the extreme end, where he met with a stronger door, which occasioned him no small manual exercise to unclose, when, to his surprise, a violent scream rung upon his ears; and, as he threw open the arched door, he beheld his terrified party, who, awaked by the noise of his forcing of the portal, had rushed into the arms of the men, to whom they clung, shrieking for protection against nothing less than a legion of armed spectres, whom their affrighted fancies had in an instant conjured from their graves.

'I have,' said Sir Thomas, 'explored the chief apartments of the abbey, and rejoice to find them every way beyond my expectations. Workmen, and other necessary persons shall be instantly engaged for the repair of this ancient and long-neglected mansion, which, as I mean to make it perfectly habitable, I have now only to assure all present, that the seat of my family has nothing to excite just terror, or encourage misconceptions relating to beings that never had existence.'

As soon as their small repast was ended, Sir Thomas desired Owen to take one of the horses, and find the nearest way to the next town; for a supply of food was become necessary. Sir Thomas went, followed by Owen, round the southern angle of the abbey, where they had a full view of a portal more ruinous than the one they had quitted, and which presented a long and dreary continuation of those parts of the building once dedicated to conventual occupation, and were now crumbling into dust. 'Now,' said Sir Thomas, 'mount your horse, and proceed down yonder avenue, which will conduct you to the next town; and likewise inquire for one Norman Clare, who was steward to these estates; explain to him my present situation, and that I require his attendance; and give him full commission to engage such workmen as shall be needful for the full repair.'

Owen immediately obeyed; and lashing his steed into a fast trot, soon arrived within sight of a poor but neat-looking cottage, with a venerable looking old man sitting beneath a spreading oak, who had seen the intruder as he galloped out of the forest, with surprise strongly marked in his face. 'Pray,' said Owen, as he rode up to the cottage, 'can you inform me if there be one Norman Clare living in this neighbourhood?'

The old man started back with increased surprise, exclaiming, 'And pray what is thy business with Norman Clare?' 'The simple-hearted Owen entered into a full detail of his mission, adding, 'if such a person as Norman was alive, his master, Sir Thomas, Lord of Fitz-Martin's abbey and lands, demanded his assistance at the above named mansion.'

'If thou requirest to be acquainted with him, thou shalt not further waste thy labour; for truly I am Norman Clare; and since I find thou art real flesh and blood, thou shalt enter with me my lonely dwelling, and welcome shalt thou be to share its homely fare.' Owen alighted joyfully from his panting steed, and entered with his host the well-arranged cottage. 'Here, good dame!' exclaimed Norman to his aged partner, 'I have brought you a stranger, who, coming from the old abbey yonder, must needs lack something to cheer his spirits.'

Owen then entered at large upon the whole of his late journey, and its termination at the abbey.

'What!' cried Blanche, 'lie in such a place as the haunted abbey! Mercy on us! friend, does your master know that it has not been inhabited for more than an hundred years; and does he not know that it is all over so full of goblins and spectres, that nobody will ever set a foot near it? And, moreover, the ghost of Anna is seen every night, walking down the great long aisles of the church up to the altar, where it kneels till the clock strikes twelve, when it goes out of the great doors, which fly open at its approach, and walks to the great south tower, where it utters three loud shrieks; when the old wicked Baron's ghost is forced to come, as soon as these are heard; and Anna drives him with a fire-brand in one hand, and a dead child in the other, all over the ruins, till they come to the chamber where the Baron used to sleep after he treacherously got possession of the abbey. Dismal yells, and dying groans, are then heard to echo through all the apartments, and blazing lights thrown about the great north bed-chamber, till the great turret clock, that has never for many a weary long year been touched by mortal hands, tolls heavily two, and sometimes three strokes upon the bell.'

'Nonsense, nonsense,' interrupted Norman, with a wink, meant to silence the loquacity of Blanche, 'you see all these idle terrors are done away. Did not Sir Thomas and his family sleep there last night, and is not Mr Owen here alive to tell us so?' Poor Owen, a coward at heart, sat trembling every joint as he listened to the extravagances of Blanche, and gave implicit belief to all the wild incoherences she tittered. At length, Owen, aided by a flagon of ale, which inspired him with something like resolution, once more braved the terrific dangers of the abbey, and mounting his horse, (well stored with many comforts provided by Norman,) he galloped down the avenue leading towards the abbey.

The next day, Norman, followed by a parcel of workmen, brought with him all his paper accounts, and monies, the produce of the rents, which he had faithfully hoarded up for the lord of the demesne whenever he thought proper to claim it.

One half of the range of the west front in a month's time was rendered perfectly safe; and having undergone a complete repair, the apartments soon began to lose much of their desolate and forlorn appearance. Three chambers were fitted up for the future residence of the steward; but it was a work of long entreaty before Sir Thomas could prevail on the venerable old Norman to take possession of them.

The lovely Rosaline (the Baron's only daughter) had at this period arrived at the age of sixteen, and having no society, but the inmates of the abbey, nor accustomed to any other, would dispense with the forms of rank, and, seating herself by the brisk wood fire that blazed on the hearth, listen attentively to the talkative Blanche's terrible narratives of spectres and supernatural appearances.

Rosaline would, at times, anxiously attend to these dreadful stories; as the tales of Blanche were generally terrific in the extreme, and always finished with the history of the Baron and the nun; who, she affirmed, still haunted the ruins of the abbey. The story of Sister Anna had made a deep impression on her memory; and having often wished for a clear and true account of what was the end of the unfortunate nun, had determined to search among the ruins, in hopes that some discoveries might be made, that would lead to a development of her death. But as this enterprise could not so well be performed alone, she made Jannette her confidant, who readily promised obedience.

As they proceeded from the abbey, Rosaline failed not to examine every nook and corner that crossed her way. Sometimes she ventured up the broken steps of a broken tower, whose lofty battlements no longer reared their proud heads, that lay extended in the area. She ascended the first story, and through the heavy arch had a full view of the south tower. Rosaline bade Jannette observe it, and asked if she had courage to enter it.--'Indeed, my lady,' she replied, 'I never behold that tower, but it makes me tremble. It was there, they say, that poor Anna was confined; and I dare hardly look at it. Besides, my lady, you see it is more ruinous than this; nor is it safe to be approached. Surely, Madam, you do not mean to make the trial?'

'If, as you say, that was the prison of poor Anna, it is there only I may hope to find some documents relative to her fate. I am, therefore, resolved to proceed. But for you, Jannette, stay where you are: I shall not require a further attendance than your remaining within hearing.'

Rosaline descended the broken steps, and proceeded towards the tower, whilst Jannette, not daring to advance, stood trembling, entreating her young lady to forego her dangerous enterprise: but Rosaline having as yet found nothing to gratify her search, resolved not to yield to the light fears of Jannette: she therefore proceeded, and arrived at the full sight of the south tower: its black and frowning aspect, together with its weak, tottering situation, at first aroused a momentary feeling of terror; but youthful hope encouraged her to venture, and she approached the old

Gothic door, which gave her a sight of an iron grating that was fixed in the wall.

To the left she beheld a flight of stairs that led to the upper stories; but these were too weak to admit her ascent in safety to the top; she therefore gave over the design, and turned again to the iron grating. As she caught the first view of the alarming objects within, her mind, unprepared for the sudden shock, endured a momentary suspension, and she fell, nearly fainting, against the wall.

The power of calling for aid was gone, and, for a few seconds, she was unable to support herself.

The terrific spectacle that had so powerfully affected Rosaline, as she caught a view of the interior of this forlorn ruin, was a deep narrow cell, whose walls were hung with mouldering trappings of black. The only light that was admitted within, proceeded from an iron grate fixed in the amazing thickness of the wall. Around this gloomy place were fixed, in all directions, the horrific emblems of death; and which ever way the desolate inhabitant of this dreary cell turned, images of horror, shocking to nature, met the tortured view, in the terrific state and eyeless sockets of the ghastly skull bones that hung in grim appalling array. In the middle of the cell, upon a raised pedestal, stood the mouldering relics of a coffin, which had been once covered with a velvet pall, but which now hung in tatters down its sides. At one corner was a small hillock, that appeared the sad resting place of the distracted penitent; for that this was the severe prison of penance and contrition, every superstitious emblem of monkish torture that surrounded the walls plainly bore testimony of. A crucifix, and broken hour-glass, still remained, covered with dust, upon a small altar, beneath an arched recess; whilst the floor was strewed with skulls and human bones.

After the first momentary shock had subsided, Rosaline arose, and stood irresolute to proceed in researches. Her alarms were strong, but her curiosity was, if possible, stronger. She felt she should never be able voluntarily again to enter this tremendous place; and she debated whether her courage would support her, should she pursue further the daring adventure. 'Perhaps,' said she, 'this was, indeed, the final end of the unhappy sister. Alas! poor unfortunate, this too, surely was alike your prison, and the cause of your lingering death. Yet wherefore am I thus anxious to solve the mystery of her death? Dare I lift the pall from that horrific spectacle? What if my spirits fail me, and I sink, overcome with dread, in this charnel house of death. May not my senses forsake me in the trial? or is it not very likely that terror may bereave me of my reason?--Shall I enter?'

Either her senses were indeed confused, or perhaps her mind, wrought to a certain pitch, led her to fancy more than reality; for, as the last word dropped from her lips, she started, and thought she heard it feebly repeated by an unknown voice, which slowly pronounced, 'Enter!'

Rosaline trembled, and not exactly aware of her intentions, unfastened the grate, and threw back the rattling chains that were hooked on the staples without the cell. The grate opened with ease, and swung on its hinges with little or no resistance; and Rosaline, with an imagination distempered, and misled by the hopes of discovering something she came in search of, that would repay her fears, descended the indented declivity, and with trembling steps staggered two or three paces from the grating; but again became irresolute, and terrified from her purpose, she stopped.

'Dare I,' she faintly ejaculated, 'dare I raise the mysterious lid of that horrific coffin?'

'Dare to do so!' replied a voice, that sounded hollow along the dreaded vault; and Rosaline, whose terror now had suspended the faculty of feeling, though not of life, actually moved towards the coffin, as if performing some dreadful rite, that she found she had not a power to resist.

Impelled with a notion of that superior agency which she dared not disobey, and not exactly sensible of what she did, she fearfully cast aside the lid, which, as she touched, fell crumbling to the ground; and turning aside her head, her hand fell within the coffin; and in her fright she grasped something moist and clammy, which she brought away. Shrieking wildly, she rushed from the scene of terror, and precipitating herself through the tower-gate, fell fainting into the arms of Jannette; who, pale and terrified, called aloud for help, as she supported her insensible lady.

Norman, who had long been impatient at the stay of his mistress, and alarmed for her safety, was hastening down the ruins, when the cries of Jannette assailed his ears, and had arrived at the scene of terror as Rosaline began to open her eyes.

'Holy Virgin protect the lady,' he exclaimed. 'Hast thou seen any thing? or do these pale looks proceed from some fall which may have bruised thy tender form among the ruins?'

'Oh no, good Norman, not so,' feebly and wildly ejaculated Rosaline. 'The tower! the dreadful tower!'

'The tower! sayst thou, my' lady? Mercy on me! Have you been so hardy as to venture into that dismal place!'

Rosaline, as she gradually recovered, felt a perfect recollection of the late horrid scene, and recalling the awful voice she had heard, which she doubted not proceeded from some supernatural agency, she no sooner beheld Norman, than she darted towards her chamber, regardless of the terrors of the old steward or Jannette.

As soon as she entered her room, she drew from the folds of her robe the relics she had unknowingly grasped from the coffin. On examination, it seemed to be some folded papers; but in so decayed a condition, that they threatened to drop in pieces with the touch.

She carefully unfolded the parcel, and found it to contain the story of the unfortunate Anna; but many of the lines were totally extinct, and only here and there a few that could be distinguished.

At length, in another packet she discovered a more perfect copy of the preceding ones, which, from the style of its writing, evidently proved them to be the labour of some of the monks, who had, from the papers discovered in the cell of her confinement, been enabled to trace the truth of her melancholy story and sufferings, in which the Baron was but too principally concerned.

Rosaline, retrimming her lamp, and seating herself nearer the table, took up the monk's copy, and began, not without difficulty, to read the melancholy story of The Bleeding Nun of St Catherine's. It was in the reign of Edward the First, that, in an old dilapidated mansion, lived the poor but proud Sir Emanfred, descended of an illustrious house, whose noble progenitors had with the Conqueror settled in England, upon the establishment of their royal master.

In the two succeeding centuries, however, great changes had taken place, and many events had reduced the once powerful and splendid ancestors of Sir Emanfred to little more than a military dependence. The proud nature of the Knight shrunk from the consequences of the total ruin of his house; and, indignant at the disgraceful and humiliating change of his circumstances, he hastily quitted the gay triumphs of the British court, because his fallen fortunes and wasted patrimony no longer enabled him to vie, in the splendour of his appearance and expenditure, with the rest of the nobles of the kingdom. In the gloomy shades of his forsaken mansion, he buried himself from all the joys of social intercourse: nor was his melancholy habitation ever after disturbed by the sounds of festive cheerfulness, or the smile of contentment. Morose in temper from his disappointments of fortune, and too proud to stoop to such honourable recourses, as might have in time procured for him the re-establishment of his decayed house, he disdained all pecuniary acquirements, and determined to build his hope of future greatness on an alliance of his only child with the splendid and noble lord of Osmand. But the lovely Anna, brought up in total seclusion, and unacquainted with the manners of the world, happily free from the ambitious and haughty passions of her stern sire, had unconsciously rendered obedience to his commands impossible, and shrunk in horror from the dreaded proposal of an union with Lord Osmand; for, alas! she had not a heart to bestow, nor a hand to give away.' Anna, the beautiful and enchanting Anna, whose years scarce numbered seventeen, had known the exquisite pain and pleasures of a secret love; and, in the simple innocence of an unsuspecting mind, had given her heart, her soul, her all to a--Stranger.

Anna had never known a mother's tenderness, nor experienced a father's sheltering protection; the artless dictates of her too susceptible heart were her only guides and monitors; and, during the long absence of her sire, her soul first felt the pleasing emotions of love for an unknown but graceful Stranger, whom she had first beheld in the shades of a melancholy but romantic wood, that adjoined equally her father's domain, and the vast forest of St Catherine's monastery, where she had often been accustomed to roam, and where she had first met the fascinating Vortimer, who but too soon betrayed the unconscious maid into a confession that his fervent love was not displeasing, and that to him, and him only, she had resigned her heart, beyond even a wish for its recall. The mind of Anna was incapable of restraining the soft, thrilling ecstasies of a first infant passion. The Stranger urged his suit with all the melting, all the prevailing, eloquence of an enraptured lover, and all the outward blandishments of feeling and sincerity.

Unacquainted with the world's deceits, poor Anna listened to his fervent vows with downcast, blushing timidity, and pleased acceptance. Each secret meeting more firmly linked her chains: her very soul was devoted to the Stranger, whom, as yet, she knew not by any other title than the simple name of Vortimer.

In a moment fatally destructive to her repose, when love had blinded reason, and the artless character of Anna but too successfully aided the purposes of the Stranger, he obtained not only complete possession of her affections, but of her person also.

At midnight, in the ruined chapel of Sir Emanfred's gloomy edifice, the Stranger had prevailed on the innocent Anna to meet him, and ratify his wishes. A monk of a distant convent waited in the chapel; and the inauspicious nuptials were performed; and Anna became a bride, without knowing by what title she must in future call herself.

Scarcely had three months of happiness and love passed over her head, when a storm, dreadful and unexpected, threatened for ever to annihilate the bright prospect of felicity.

The sudden arrival of a hasty messenger from the Knight alarmed the trembling Anna; and scarce had she perused the purport of his arrival, than with a faint shriek, and a stifled cry of agony, she fell to the ground, as she feebly exclaimed, 'Lost, undone, and wretched Anna! destruction and death await thee!'

The Stranger read the fatal paper that contained the harsh mandate of his Anna's father: his brow became contracted, and his countenance overcast with apparent gloom and sorrow, as he perused the unwelcome information of the Knight's arrival, on the morrow, at his castle, to celebrate the nuptials of his daughter with the lord of Osmand, who accompanied him. For a time a gloomy silence pervaded his lips; and Anna vainly cast her tearful, imploring eyes to him for succour and protection. At length, starting from a deep reverie, he caught her in his arms, as she was sinking to the ground, and kissing her cold and quivering lips, bade her take comfort, and abide with patience the arrival of her sire; adding, that in three weeks he would return, and openly claim her as his wife; when the mystery that had so long enveloped his name and title in secrecy should be unravelled, and his adored Anna be restored to affluence and splendour. Again embracing her, he hurried precipitately from the place; and Anna--the ruined, hapless Anna--never saw him more--

.   .   .   .   .   .

Here many lines became defaced, as the ink had rotted through the vellum, and all traces of writing were totally lost in mildew and obscurity. At length she was able to continue as follows:

Ferocious rage filled the soul of the Knight, and darkened his features, as prostrate at his feet lay, overwhelmed in grief and tears, the imploring Anna. 'Spare me!' she cried, 'Oh, sire! spare your wretched child--she cannot marry the lord of Osmand!'

Fury flashed in the eyes of the stern Sir Emanfred, on hearing these words of his daughter. At length the burst of rage found vent, he seized the arm of the trembling Anna, and placing her hand forcibly in that of Sir Osmand's, commanded her to prepare herself, in three days, to become his bride, or meet the curses of an angry father, and be driven from his sight for ever.

Driven to despair, and now vainly calling on the mysterious Stranger to shield her from the direful fate that awaited her, or the still more dreadful vengeance of her unrelenting father, the hapless Anna wildly flew to the gloomy wood, in the forlorn hope that there, once more, she might behold the lord of all her love and fondest wishes. In three weeks he had promised to reclaim her; but, alas! they had already expired, and no Stranger had appeared. The fourth week of his absence came: it passed away, but he came not; and now but three days remained between her and her hateful nuptials. Wildly she wandered through the gloomy wood, and vainly cast her eyes in hopeless anguish on all around her: no Stranger met her sight: he came not to rescue his forlorn bride from the rude grasp of impending misery and destruction. Night came on; the hours passed away unheeded, yet still she quitted not the solemn shades of the dreary grove. The bell of midnight sounded; she started at the melancholy toll, and fear and awe possessed her sickening fancy. She hurried through the wood, and reached in silence her chamber; but sleep visited not the wretched Anna.

Again, as the hour of suffering drew still nigher, she threw herself in supplication before the gloomy Knight, and besought him to spare her but one week longer, ere he linked her to misery and woe; hoping by this delay to procure time for the Stranger, and give him yet another chance, ere it was too late, to save her, and claim his affianced bride. But, inexorably bent on the union of his child with Lord Osmand, the Knight, in anger, cast her from his knees, and threatened to overwhelm her with his most tremendous curses, if she did not meet Lord Osmand at the altar before the sixth hour of the early morrow had chimed upon the bell.

Poor Anna shrunk from the angry glances of the enraged Knight; despair and anguish seized her soul. The Stranger never came; he had forgotten his solemn vows, neglected his promise, and abandoned her to her fate. Whither could she fly? How was she to avoid the choice of miseries that equally pursued her? Either she must perjure her soul to false oaths, or meet the dreadful alternative of a parent's dire malediction.--Oh! whither, lost and wretched Anna! canst thou fly!

Upon the pillow of her tear-bedewed couch she vainly laid her head, to seek a momentary oblivion of her sorrow in repose. Something lay upon her pillow--It was a paper curiously folded.--With fearful, trembling expectation she hastily opened the envelope, and read, 'The Stranger guards his love; and though unseen, and yet forbidden, to reclaim his lovely bride, now watches over her safety, and awaits the precious moment when he shall hasten on the wings of love to restore his Anna to happiness and liberty. If then she would preserve herself for her unknown friend, let her instantly fly to the monastery of St Catherine's, where she may remain in security till demanded by her adoring VORTIMER.'

The unhappy maid perused the fatal lines with unsuspecting belief and joyful ecstasy; and, in compliance with the Stranger's mysterious warning, escaped at midnight from her father's mansion; and took refuge in the cloisters of St Catherine.

The haughty lady abbess received the forlorn wanderer with cold civility and suspicious scrutiny. The unfortunate Anna had, in the simple innocence of her heart, confided to the superior her mournful tale, nor left one circumstance untold that could excite her pity, save her marriage with the Stranger, for whom she now began to feel unusual fears, and dreadful forebodings of evil to herself; for a month had glided away at the abbey, and yet he came not.

The Knight, with dreadful rage, discovered his daughter's flight; but vainly sought again to restore her to his power. He never saw her more; nor knew the sad conclusion of the unhappy Anna's destiny; who, deceived and terrified by the threats, expostulations, and commands, of the lady abbess, and the father confessors of the monastery, was at length betrayed into her own destruction; for the merciless abbess threatened to return her to her lord, and to her father, if she longer refused to take the vow of monastic life.

Despair and horror now seized the suffering victim of bigotry and paternal tyranny. Another and another month elapsed, and hope no longer could support her--the cruel Stranger never came. At the gates of her prison, she was told, waited her father, with a powerful band, to force her from the abbey into the arms of a hated husband; and only the alternative of instantly taking the veil, could save her from the misery that pursued her. In a wild agony of terror, that had totally bereft her of her reason, she faintly bade them save her from her father's vengeance.

That instant the sacred, irrevocable vow was administered, and all its binding forms complied with by the lost St Anna, who, in the terror of her father, had for a moment forgot her previous engagements with the Stranger-- forgot that she must, in a little time, become, perhaps, a wretched mother, and now was a still more wretched nun.

.   .   .   .   .   .

Here again the papers were totally useless, as Rosaline could only make out here and there a word, by which it appeared, that the Baron Fitzmartin had accused the order, with breaking the vow of celibacy. At length she read as follows:

With difficulty he was prevailed upon to suspend his proceedings against the abbey till the succeeding morrow, whilst the holy sisterhood endured the most persecuting examination from the lady abbess. No signs of guilt, however, were found; and the fathers, rejoicing in their expected security, were debating on an ample defiance to the Baron, when news was brought that Sister St Anna had fallen senseless on the steps of the grand altar, and had been with difficulty removed to her cell. Thither the abbess instantly hastened; and as the insensible nun lay still reclined on her mattress, her outer garment unlaced to admit of respiration, the disfigurement of her person first forcibly struck the lady mother with suspicion. She started, frowned; then looked again; conviction flashed upon her eyes; and, regardless of pity for the still lifeless state of the hapless Anna, she commanded all to quit the cell, and send instantly the father abbot to her. The father hastily obeyed, and entered. The lady abbess murmured in a hollow voice, as frowns of fury darted from her now terrific countenance: 'Behold the guilty wretch that, with impious sacrilege, hath defiled our holy sanctuary, and brought destruction on the glory of our house's fame!--Say, holy father, how must we dispose of the accursed apostate?'

Before the abbot could reply, the unfortunate Anna awoke from the counterfeit of death's repose, and, wildly casting her eyes around her cell, beheld the forms of her inveterate destroyers.

Their fierce and angry looks of dreadful inquiry were bent upon the terrified nun, who, sickened with an unusual apprehension and dismay, whilst the abbot, fixing on the trembling Anna an increasing look of penetrating sternness, in a hollow, deep-toned voice, that sunk to her appalled heart, thus exclaimed: 'What punishment too terrible can await that guilty wretch who with sacrilege defiles our holy order?--say, lost one of God, art thou not guilty?'

Sinking on her knees, of every hope of life bereft, the unhappy Anna drooped her head to avoid the terrible scrutiny of truths pronounced, and looks unanswerable. No chance of escape was left her; she dared not prevaricate; and only with a groan of agony she feebly exclaimed--'I am, indeed!--Have mercy, holy father, as you shall hereafter expect to receive mercy from our heavenly Judge, on my involuntary crime!' She then turned to the frowning abbess her beseeching eyes, and piteously added, as she clung around her knees, 'Spare, oh gracious mother, spare a repentant daughter!'

In the countenances of her terrific judges poor Anna read the horrid mandate of her fate; for against the sacred order of the sisterhood she had sinned beyond atonement by any other punishment than death--Death the most horrible and excruciating! Vainly then she knelt, and clung to the robe of the abbess; she had slandered with sacrilege the purity of God's anointed house; its ministers and sacred devotees were sullied with a stain, that only the blood of a victim could wash away. Nor was the plea of marriage to a knight, who evidently never meant to claim her, admitted as the slightest expiation of her perjured vows to the abbey, and the disgrace she had brought on its sanctified inmates. Her horrid crimes demanded instant punishment: and the dreadful vengeance of the insulted members of the church could only be appeased by the immediate extirpation of the heinous apostate. To dispose of the unfortunate nun for ever, beyond the possibility of her being produced as a living evidence of the Baron's censure, and the abbey's shame, was now become an event absolutely necessary to the safety and welfare of the order: the claims of mercy, or the melting pleadings of pity, were alike disregarded for the stronger interest of the more immediate triumph of the abbey over its avowed and implacable enemy: and the father abbot, with the lady mother, having exhausted on the lost fair one the dreadful thunders of the church's vengeance, forcibly tore themselves from her distracted grasp, and prepared to inflict the terrific punishments that awaited their despairing victim, who, shrieking vainly for aid, and calling piteously on the Stranger for rescue and protection from her horrid fate, was borne by the tormentors from her cell to the dungeon of the south tower.

At the hour of midnight they dragged the miserable victim from her bed, and deep in the horrific dungeons of the prison plunged the distracted nun!--Groans, sighs, and shrieks, alternately rung echoing round the rugged walls: the torturing horrors of famine awaited the unfortunate nun; no pity alleviated her misery; and in the centre of the place stood the coffin destined for her; whilst round the walls and floor, in all directions, were strewed the ghastly ensigns of woe and torment.

ANONYMOUS

A faint glimmering lamp, suspended from the massy bars of the roof (as if with a refinement of cruelty unequalled, to blast the sight of the victim, and shut out every contemplation but her immediate fate) served to shew her the horrors that overwhelmed her, and the terrific engines of her tortures. The implements of confession were placed on the lid of her coffin; for the fathers denied her even the last consolation of absolution; but these she only in moments of short intellect would use, when distracted sentences, and wild, unfinished exclamations and appeals were all that it produced, sufficiently depictive of the horrors of her fate.

Two days of lingering sufferings had passed, and the third was nearly closed. Shut from life, and light, and every means of existence, the pangs of hunger seized the frantic sufferer, and the perils of premature childbirth writhed her anguished frame. Shrieks of despair rang through the building, and echoed to the vault of heaven. Hark! again that soul-appalling cry!--Inhuman fiends, is mercy dead within you!--Is there no touch of pity in your obdurate souls!--And thou too, remorseless betrayer of trusting innocence, hear ye not yon soul-appalling cry of her thy fatal love has destroyed?--Hark! again she calls on thy unpitying name; and now, in the bitterness of her soul's sufferings, she curses thee, and imprecates heaven's just vengeance on thy perjured head! Heaven hears the awful appeal!--it will avenge thee, suffering Anna! Now sink to death appeased.--Again the shrieks--Sure it is her last! The holy sisterhood, appalled, fly wildly from the dreadful tower; but vainly supplicate the mercy of their superiors for its dying inmate. Nature is exhausted, and hark, again the groans grow fainter! Short-breathed murmurs proclaim the welcome dissolution of life. The soul, though confined with the suffering frame within the massy bars of her prison, at length has burst its bonds--It mounts from death, and in a moment is freed for ever. A short prayer addressed to the throne of mercy, releases the sufferer, and wafts her soul from the persecution of the wicked. The cruel strife has ceased--Poor Anna is at rest--her voice is heard no more. In the coffin of penitence she laid her suffering form; perhaps, it will never be removed from thence. Her guilty judges tremble at the place, nor dare their unhallowed footsteps approach the sacred dust.

Again the papers were useless, but it seemed, by what she could make out, that the haughty Baron triumphed over the Fathers of the Abbey, to the entire seclusion of the order. At length she came to the following passage, which concluded the manuscript.

The vengeance of heaven hung heavily over the conscience of the wicked Baron, nor was he suffered ever after to partake of happiness. It was on the third evening after his removal from his castle to the abbey he had plundered, that, retiring earlier than usual to his unwelcome couch, he tried in the arms of sleep to lose the remembrance of his crimes, and the terrible vengeance they inflicted on his guilty conscience. The sullen bell had tolled the hour of midnight ere he could compose his mind to repose. On this night, however, unusual restlessness pervaded his frame; nor could he for some time close in forgetfulness his eye-lids. At length a kind of unwilling stupor lulled for a moment his tortured spirits, and he slept. Not long did the balmy deity await him: troubled groans of anguish sounded through the apartment, and piercing shrieks rung bitterly in his ears. Starting in horror, he wildly raised himself, half bent, on his couch, and drew aside his curtains. The chamber was in total darkness, and every taper seemed suddenly to have been extinguished. At that moment the heavy bell of the abbey clock struck one. A freezing awe stole over the senses of the Baron: he in vain attempted to call his attendants; for speech was denied him; and a suspense of trembling horror had chilled his soul. His blood ran cold to its native source; his hair stood erect, and his countenance was distorted; for, as his eyes turned wildly, he beheld, standing close to the side of his bed, the pale figure of a female form, thinly clothed in the habiliments of a nun, and bearing in one hand a taper, whilst the other arm supported the ghastly form of a dead infant reclining on her breast. The countenance of the figure was pale, wan, and horrible to behold; for from its motionless eyes no spark of life proceeded; but they were fixed in unmoving terrific expression on the appalled Baron. At length a hollow-sounding voice pronounced through the closed lips of the spectre, 'O false, false Vortimer! accursed and rejected of thy Maker! knowest thou not the shadowy form that stands before thee? knowest thou not thy wretched bride? seest thou not the murdered infant thou hast destroyed?--From the deep bosom of immensity, the yawning horrors of the grave, the spirit of St Anna comes to call for vengeance and retribution; for know, the curses of her latest moments, when writhing beneath the agonies, the torments of death, and devouring hunger, that she then called upon thy head, were heard; and never shalt thou, guilty wretch! enjoy one quiet moment more. My mangled form, as now thou seest me, and dreams for ever of affright and terror, shall haunt thy thoughts with horror; nor shall even the grave rescue thee from the tortures I await to inflict.-- Farewell--farewell till next we meet. In the grove where first thy perjured soul won on my happy, unsuspecting nature, and drew my youthful heart from parental duty and obedience, there shalt thou again behold me!'

Suddenly the eyes of the spectre became animated--Oh! then what flashes of appalling anger darted their orbits on the horror-struck Vortimer! three dreadful shrieks rung pealing through the chamber, now filled with a blaze of sulphurous light. The spectre suddenly became invisible, and the Baron fell senseless on his couch.

The Mysterious Spaniard

by Anonymous

THE Chevalier Franval, and his sister Amarylla, were the only children of a French General of great reputation, who died at the beginning of the last century, at an elegant villa to which he had retired in the evening of his days, at the distance of a few leagues from the city of Paris.

At the time of her father's death, Amarylla was receiving her education in the convent of St. Ann at Aurillac. The Chevalier watched the death-bed of his parent with the most anxious and tender affection; and the most solemn injunction which that parent bestowed on him, was, to supply his place, by every care and attention in his power, to his orphan sister; a command so congenial to the feelings of the Chevalier, that it was a satisfaction to himself to pronounce a vow to this effect on the ear of his expiring father.

Six months after the death of the General, was the time appointed for Amarylla to quit her convent; and the period being arrived, her brother set out for Aurillac, resolved himself to be her protector on her journey home. He travelled leisurely, and stopping one evening in a small town, where he was informed that the church was a handsome structure, he strolled towards it, intending to amuse an hour by viewing it. On his return to his inn, he perceived loitering before it, a gentleman whom he had seen examining the beauties of the church at the same time that he had been engaged in observing them himself; and concluding that he was a stranger in the place, and his fellow lodger at the inn, addressed himself to him. The young man (for he did not appear above twenty years of age) met Franval's advances towards an acquaintance with evident pleasure, and entered into conversation with him in a manner which displayed him to have added a liberal education to a good natural understanding. He proved (as Franval had supposed) to be a lodger at the same inn, and they agreed to sup together. The stranger informed Franval, that he was a Spaniard by birth; his name Don Manuel di Vadilla; and that he was travelling, attended by only one servant, solely for his amusement and improvement. After an evening pleasantly spent by both parties, they separated for the night; and on the following morning, took a friendly leave of each other previously to pursuing their respective journeys.

The conciliating manners of Don Manuel had made a very favourable impression in his behalf on the mind of the Chevalier; and often, as he rode along, did he reflect on the agreeable hours which he had passed in the society of the young Spaniard. At length he reached the convent of Saint Ann, where a meeting of the most joyful and affectionate nature took place between him and his sister.

Amarylla had always been handsome whilst a girl; but during the four years that her brother had been separated from her, he beheld a great augmentation of her charms to have taken place. She was become tall and graceful; her eyes were of a sparkling blue, and expressive of the sweetness of her disposition; her cheeks, twin roses; her lips a bed of coral, within which reposed a double row of pearls.

After remaining three days at Aurillac, the Chevalier and his sister commenced their journey towards home. As they travelled, he remarked that Amarylla, notwithstanding the sweetness of her temper, which was never for a moment interrupted, appeared to have some object, either of regret or melancholy, for her private thoughts. She would frequently fall into short fits of absence, and heave sighs, which appeared to be accompanied with some tender emotion. The Chevalier entreated her, by the love which he bore her, as the only remnant of his revered parents, to confide to him the secrets of her heart. For some time Amarylla, with blushes, evaded a direct reply: at length she confessed that a young man, of whom she had a few weeks before caught an accidental view from the seat appointed in the chapel of her convent for the boarders, had made an impression on her heart, which she could not obliterate from it.

Her brother smiled at the warmth of the innocent Amarylla's first sensation of the imperious passion of love, and told her, that as her acquaintance with society increased, which it would do as soon as she was introduced, on her return home, to the world, she would herself laugh at the serious manner in which she now treated a recollection of this nature.

In apologizing for her confession, Amarylla urged that the youth had beheld her, not withstanding her retired situation; and that his eyes had beamed with an expression which had eloquently declared his wish of approaching her; and that he had left the church with a last gaze, which she had understood as entreating her to remember him. Still the Chevalier continued to smile, and Amarylla to sigh.

A journey free from all disasters brought them to the Chevalier's villa: it was the family mansion, a house of considerable elegance, and furnished in a style of magnificence which rivalled those of most of the nobles: in particular, one of its saloons, and a breakfast apartment on the second story, which were ornamented with paintings of so great value and excellence as frequently to attract strangers to inspect them; an indulgence which was always readily granted to persons of a respectable rank.

On entering the house, the Chevalier was met by his housekeeper, who informed him, that he had a gentleman, a stranger, lodging in one of the chambers. Franval requested an explanation of her words. She answered, that the gentleman of whom she spoke, had come to the villa about a week before, to view the pictures; that his foot having slipped as he was descending the stairs, he had had the misfortune of breaking one of his legs, and that she had been compelled by humanity, to offer him a bed in the house. The Chevalier, with the natural generosity and feeling of his heart, commended the conduct she had pursued; and, after a short time, went to visit the stranger, and make him personal offers of his services, when, to his great surprise, he beheld in the invalid, Don Manuel di Vadilla.

The nature of their remarks on this extraordinary meeting may be easily imagined: nor can it be doubted, that the Chevalier caused every attention to be paid to the recovery of a young man, his first acquaintance with whom had created for him a favourable prejudice in his heart.

Franval passed many hours in each day by the bedside of his guest; and as their acquaintance increased, he learnt from him the following particulars of his history: that he was an orphan; that the few relatives whom he possessed, were all distant ones; that Spain was a country of which the manners and the inhabitants were not congenial to his feelings, and that he had therefore quitted it, and resolved to settle in France; but he had not yet fixed on any spot as a residence: that his fortune, which was ample, he had placed in the hands of a banker in Paris; and had a servant, who was his only attendant, a man apparently about forty-five years of age, named Rodalvo, to whom he expressed himself particularly attached, as he had been in his service from the hour of his birth.

In their conversation, one day, it chanced that Franval mentioned to Don Manuel, his having brought home his sister from the convent of Saint Ann at Aurillac. At the name of the convent the Spaniard smiled; and when Franval enquired the cause of his doing so, he confessed to him, that, having one evening attended vespers in the Chapel of that convent, he had been particularly struck by the beauty of one of the boarders; that, at the time, he had not believed the impression made by her charms on his heart to have been so deep as he had since found it; but that with each succeeding day, he now desired more earnestly to see her again.

The Chevalier recollected the confession which his sister had made to him, of her having beheld with the eye of partiality, a stranger in the church of Saint Ann, who she believed had viewed her with the same emotions as she had seen him; and from the similarity of her account to that of the young Spaniard, he doubted not that they were reciprocally the hero and heroine of each others' adventures. He buried his suspicions in his breast but the progress of time proved them to have been correct.

When Don Manuel was sufficiently recovered from his hurt to quit his chamber, and descend into the apartments in the daily use of the family, the first moment of his encountering Amarylla, was attended with an emotion of joy and surprise on the part of each, which clearly explained to Franval the justice of his conjectures. The enamoured pair were in raptures at this unexpected introduction to each other; and when the perfect use of Don Manuel's limbs was again restored to him, he still lingered at the villa of the Chevalier Franval, unable to quit the adorable object who possessed his heart.

Thus passed on six months, at the expiration of which, Amarylla requested her brother's permission to bestow her hand on Don Manuel. The Chevalier saw that her affections were placed on him, and that he appeared devoted to her. He had now gained, he believed, a thorough knowledge of Don Manuel's heart and principles; he regarded them calculated to ensure happiness to his beloved sister; and their union was accordingly sanctioned by his approbation.

Never were two amiable hearts more happy than were those of Don Manuel and his Amarylla in the possession of each other; and the Chevalier Franval, unwilling to lose the pleasure of their society, invited them to make his villa their abode. Two years rolled on in happiness uninterrupted, during the course of which two lovely infants strengthened the bond of affection between their parents. Shortly after the birth of their second child, Don Manuel, one morning at breakfast, expressed an intention of riding that day to Paris, and returning again in the evening: this was by no means an unusual thing either with him or his brother-in-law Franval; and when the coffee was removed, he set out for the metropolis, attended by his servant Rodalvo.

The evening closed without the return of Don Manuel; the night advanced, and still he did not arrive. His wife consoled herself with the idea that some engagement, which he had been unable to decline, might have detained him to sleep at Paris, and that the morning would bring him home; but alas! her hope was fallacious; the morning came unaccompanied by Don Manuel; and once more the veil of night descended to the earth, without witnessing his return to his disconsolate Amarylla.

The Chevalier Franval was not less anxious for the fate of his brother-in-law, than distressed at beholding the misery which Don Manuel's mysterious absence caused his sister; and immediately repaired to Paris, to make enquiries concerning him. But in vain were all his attempts at discovering the truth; not a breath of intelligence could be obtained by him, either of Don Manuel, or his servant Rodalvo. The endeavours of the Chevalier to gain some light upon this dark occurrence, were unabating, and utterly unsuccessful. The days crept on; these grew into weeks, and still the adored husband of Amarylla did not return; and her grief and despondency were almost raised to madness.

At length a vague account reached the Chevalier and his sister, that her lost husband had been seen travelling in a carriage, which was moving at an extremely swift pace, upon one of the high roads at the southern extremity of the kingdom which led across the Pyrenees into Spain. From the first moment of his disappearance, Amarylla had constantly repeated her conviction, that not infidelity to her, but some misfortune, which he had not been able to counteract, had torn him from her; and she now declared her intention of endeavouring to trace his steps. With much entreaty and persuasion, her brother over-ruled her purpose, and prevailed upon her to remain the guardian of her children, whilst he undertook the office of following the track that had been described to them as the one pursued by Don Manuel.

Instant preparation was accordingly made for the Chevalier's journey, and, after a most melancholy scene of separation from his sister, he set out, accompanied by a friend named Montreville, whom he had requested to become the partner of his undertaking; and attended his Henri, a confidential servant of his own.

Their journey was pursued with the greatest alacrity till they reached the southern extremity of the kingdom: here they proceeded more slowly, being frequently delayed by their uncertainty of what road to take, and by the inquiries which they made after the object of their search. Not a gleam of success smiled on them, but still they pursued their way with unabating energy. About noon of a gloomy and uncomfortable day, they reached the foot of the rugged Pyrenees. Franval had already determined to proceed into Spain, and accordingly having refreshed themselves at an inn upon the borders of the kingdom they were about to quit, they began to ascend the rough path which led across the mountains.

They rode on till the shades of evening, which were beginning to fall on the earth, warned them to seek shelter for the night. The gloom of an overclouded sky, rendered the coming darkness more rapid than usual in its approach; and the light of day was almost entirely expelled from the Heavens, when the Chevalier Franval was so fortunate as to descry a light in a distant habitation.

"See there," he cried, on observing it, "a light at length appears! Thank Heaven, we shall now get housed for the night; for it is doubtless a post-house from whence it shines."

The light appeared in view till they were arrived within a short distance of the house, and it then vanished in a sudden manner, as if it had been blown out.

They rode up to the door: Henri applied the butt-end of his whip to it in lieu of a knocker; at the same time remarking, 'That if the inhabitants were in bed, every one could scarcely be asleep, except the lamp they had seen had gone out of itself.'

For a time they were led to conjecture that this had been the case, for no reply was returned to their repeated knockings: but at length, after another salute on the part of Henri with his leaden-headed whip upon the hollow door, which was loud enough to have raised the dead, if they were ever to be raised by mortal means, a window in the upper part of the house was opened, and a head thrust out. "What is it you want?" asked the voice of a female.

"Meat, drink, and repose," replied Montreville; "have you them to sell?"

"I am no conjurer, to sell sleep," replied the woman, in a tone between pleasantry and sulkiness. "If you mean that you want to lodge here, I have not a pallet in my house that is unoccupied;" and with these uncourteous words she drew in her head again, and shut the window.

"I wish we had not travelled so late," said Franval.

"Phoo, nonsense," cried Montreville, who was a young man, and whose good spirits, and gaiety of heart, never forsook him, "they must at all events allow us to sit up in the house, if they can't put us to bed in it. I'll be satisfied with a chair to repose in, if they will but open the larder to me."

"And the cellar, Monsieur," said Henri.

"And the cellar, as you say," replied Montreville. "So, at them again, Henri; beat another rattatatoo upon the door, and let us learn if we can't come to terms, now we agree to put beds out of the question."

Henri had again recourse to his leaden-headed whip and in about ten minutes the same casement was again opened, and the rough voice of a man called out, "Whoever ye are, if ye do not go quietly about your business, and cease to disturb the peace of my house, I'll find means to make you answer for your behaviour."

"Our business, friend, is here," replied Montreville. "We are three half-starved travellers, who request to be allowed to shelter ourselves in your house during the night."

"Half-starved travellers, indeed," grumbled out the host: "it is worth while raising a man out of his sleep, to attend to half-starved travellers, truly."

"But my friend only means," said Franval, "that we are very hungry travellers, not very poor ones; and I add in his name, and my own, that we will reward you very liberally for any accommodation you may grant us."

"Upon the word of a Christian," said Henri, "there is gold in the saddle bags of both these gentlemen."

"All the better for them," returned the host, "but as I am no robber, nor can admit them into my house, none of it is likely to fall to my share."

"Why can you not admit us?" enquired Franval. "We are not robbers any more than yourself."

"It cannot be," returned the host.

"So you have told us before," replied the Chevalier; "and still do not inform us by what motive you are actuated, in refusing us shelter beneath your roof."

The host was silent.

"Yours is a post-house, is it not?" continued Franval.

"Yes," was the reply.

"Then let me tell you, friend," rejoined Montreville, "that as you live by keeping open house, the travellers upon whom you shut your door, have a just right to receive a very good reason, for your conduct, or to open the door for themselves."

"Are ye Catholics, gentlemen?" demanded the landlord.

"Yes, we are," both answered.

"Do you respect an oath as sacred?" enquired the host.

"Yes, yes; we do, we do," replied all three; imagining that some terms for their entrance into the house were about to be proposed to them.

"Then know," replied the host, "that I have already once to-night sworn by Saint Francis not to open my door; and I now swear by him a second time, to keep my first oath sacred."

Montreville was beginning to fly into a passion. The host stopped him, by raising his voice and continuing to speak; "But if I can render you any other service; if a flask of wine, a loaf of bread, or a lanthorn to light you on your way, are of any use to you, you shall have them."

"Let us taste the wine," said Montreville, whilst Franval sat meditating on the strangeness of the host's conduct.

A flask of good wine for the production of a post-house was handed out to them, and with it some cakes of newly-baked bread. Hunger is a keen sensation, that requires much less parade in its gratification than custom usually assigns to it; and, seated upon their saddles, they found the bread and wine very refreshing and comfortable.

"You have dealt so far honourably by us," said Franval, "and shall experience the same honour from us. Here," added be, throwing a demi-louis d'or at the window as he spoke, "this for your bread and wine, and twenty more shall follow it, if you will let us in."

"It is a good price, Messieurs; but I am better paid to keep you out," said the host.

"Us!" cried Montreville, "to keep us out?"

"Not you in particular," returned the man; "for I know you not; every one, I mean."

A woman now advanced to the window with a lanthorn, which had a lamp burning in it; the man received it at her hands, and lowering it out of the casement, asked if they chose to have it?

Henri received it; and the host then drew in his head, and was upon the point of shutting the casement.

"Stay, hear us an instant, I beg," said Franval. "Cannot you direct us to any cottage, any dwellings, where we might pass the night?"

"There are stray cottages scattered about," answered the host; "but you would find it impossible to gain admittance into any one of them: their inhabitants would take you for robbers, and nothing you could say would convince them to the contrary, at this time of the night: they live in so great fear of banditti, that they might even, perhaps, fire upon you without enquiring your business."

"To cut the matter short at once," exclaimed Montreville, "tell us how much you have received to keep out visitors, and if our purse is rich enough, we will outbid your guests."

"Gentlemen," said, the host, gravely, "you said you were Catholics, and respected an oath. Remember mine--You shall not come in."

"But if the inhabitants of cottages are afraid of three men, probably those of castles will not have the same apprehensions, as they are provided both with numbers and arms; so cannot you direct us to one of them?" enquired Franval.

"Why this is a part of the country where there are but few buildings of that description," answered the host; "there is but one within ten leagues of us, and that is at the distance of nearly four from this spot; and were you near it, I would not by any means advise you to attempt to enter it."

"Why so? who inhabits it?" asked Montreville.

"He is known by the name of Don Bazilio," replied the host, "and is by some reputed to be a nobleman of great wealth; others believe him to be Belzebub himself."

Montreville laughed at the manner of the host's expressing himself; and Franval's eye was at that moment attracted by a faint light which proceeded from an upper casement of the house, at which he perceived standing, a tall, lank form, of a swarthy and terrific countenance, which almost corresponded with his idea of the being which the host had just named, and caused him an undescribable sensation for the moment he beheld it; and it was but a moment that his eye had fixed on it, ere the shutter was pulled up, and closed it from his sight.

Franval made no observation on what he had seen to his companions; and Henri, addressing the host, said, "I suppose you mean to let us understand that it is haunted."

"Dreadfully, dreadfully haunted, is the Castle of Virandola," replied the landlord; "at least so it is reported. I never went to see, nor ever intend it."

"What shall we do in this cursed dilemma?" exclaimed Montreville.

"I have done all it is in my power to do for you," said the host; "and so I wish you safe travelling; and a good night, Messieurs;" and with these words he shut the casement.

Montreville was again on the point of calling him back, when Franval stopped him, by saying, "Come, let us ride on."

"Ride on! but whither?" cried Montreville.

"We can have no choice; the road lies before us," replied Franval; then, in an under tone, he added, "I'll explain myself to you presently;" and as he spoke, he clapped spurs to his horse, and set forward; and his companions followed his example.

"Why did you so suddenly leave the house which you were a quarter of an hour ago as eager as myself to enter?" enquired Montreville of his friend, before they had ridden an hundred yards away from the post-house.

Franval did not slacken his horse's pace till Montreville a second time urged his enquiry; and Franval then replied, "I have no doubt but that the reason of our being refused admittance into that house, is, that a gang of banditti, or at least some members of a lawless community of that nature, are concealed within it; perhaps in the very act of flying from justice;" and he then described the terrific visage which he had seen peeping through the window, and which, he said, if it had been a human countenance, he could only suppose to be that of a savage and bloodthirsty plunderer.

"Thank Heaven, I did not see him," cried Henri.

"We all owe our thanks to Heaven, that we were not admitted into the house, if such are its guests, as I conjecture them to be," said Franval.

"But in my opinion," returned Montreville, "we are far from safe now: don't it appear likely to you, that we were turned from the house, in order that these fellows, of whom you saw one, might pursue and plunder, perhaps murder, us? The rascal of a host would not lose the credit of his house, by suffering us to be assailed in it, lest any of us should have the good fortune to escape from their clutches, and relate the story; so he artfully takes a deeper share in the plot, by sending us forward."

"I have no fears of that kind," rejoined Franval; "our horses are fleet-footed, and will outstrip many animals."

"Of what use is their fleetness in this gloom?" said Montreville: "don't you perceive that the night is become so dark, that when we are half a dozen paces before or behind Henri and his lanthorn, we cannot discover the road? Thus, in such an emergency, the fleetness of their feet would, in all probability, only serve to carry us headlong down a precipice. The farther we get away from the post-house, however, the better, I think; so let us lose no time in debating."

This was agreed to by Franval; and they again spurred their horses into a trot, which they continued for about half a league, when a rocky break in the ground obliged them to move with caution, and at foot's pace. Whilst they were crossing this uneven track of ground, "Hark! Messieurs, hark!" cried Henri.

"What! what do you hear?" asked Montreville impatiently.

"The trampling of horses, Messieurs: don't you?" was the reply.

"I do, I do," cried Montreville: "they are coming upon us! Franval, don't you hear them?"

A pause of silence ensued: Franval broke it: "I did hear them," he said, "but they are no longer audible."

"They have stopped," said Montreville, "perhaps till some more of their comrades have joined them."

"Or, perhaps," said Henri, "they have turned out of the road upon the grass, that we may not hear their approach: they must judge that their horses hoofs cannot escape our hearing on the beaten pathway, as our lanthorn informs them exactly at what distance we are from them."

"Oh, curse the lanthorn; blow it out," cried Montreville.

"No, no," interrupted Franval: "in the course of our necessities this night, its light may prove as beneficial to us, as we now consider it injurious to our safety; therefore give it to me, Henri, and I'll hide it under my cloak."

"The sounds do not return," said Henri.

"It is as dark as pitch," cried Montreville.

"I can distinguish a knot of trees to our right," said Franval: "my plan is, that we ride in amongst them, and keep ourselves concealed there for a short time, during which period it is not improbable that they may pass us, supposing us to be gone on.--What think you of my scheme?"

"I do not disapprove it," said Montreville; "but we will load our pistols."

"Undoubtedly," replied Franval; "but the expedient I have proposed may save us from the necessity of spilling human blood, or suffering our own to be spilt."

They rode swiftly up to the trees, which were not above two score in number, planted in a shallow declivity at the mouth of the valley. Partial clumps of underwood formed a tolerable screen between them and the road they had just quitted, and they sat scarcely allowing themselves to respire, lest the suspiration of their breath should prevent their hearing any other sound which it might be important to them not to lose.

Nearly a quarter of an hour was thus spent, without the least noise of any kind meeting their ears, when they heard a sound resembling the leaves of a bush, when pressed upon by a person who is endeavouring to force himself a passage through them.

"There, there!" whispered Montreville.

Franval cocked his pistol, but did not speak.

Several minutes again passed away in silence. "It was only the wind," again whispered Montreville; but scarcely had he spoken, ere the noise was repeated; and in the following instant a voice exclaimed, "Proceed to the Castle of Virandola."

Montreville immediately discharged his pistol towards the spot from whence the voice had proceeded, and Henri fired off his in the same direction.

When the report of the pistols had died away, universal silence again prevailed; no groan announced the bullets to have inflicted a wound: no flying step discovered the discharge of their tubes to have inspired any object with fear. "What can this mean?" exclaimed Franval.

"It is, doubtless, a lure to draw us into the power of some enemy. Ten to one but the Castle of Virandola is the residence of a banditti, who hope by this stratagem to inveigle us into their power," replied Montreville. "A likely story, indeed, that we should proceed to a place we have the account of, which the landlord gave us of this castle, upon such an obscure invitation. You would not certainly be so rash as to think of it?"

"The voice appeared more than human," said Franval.

"Nonsense," exclaimed Montreville; "I say it is some trick; and whatever your opinion may be, I swear that if I go to the castle"--

"Swear not, but go," interrupted the voice which had before been heard; and it now spoke from the opposite direction to that whence it had before proceeded.

"There again," cried Franval.

"'Tis solemn, I confess," said Montreville; "but still, I think it is mortal."

"Let us search whether we can discover some one hidden amongst the bushes," rejoined Franval, drawing the lanthorn from under his cloak; and as he spoke, he vaulted from his horse. Montreville followed his example; and Henri taking the bridles of their horses, they proceeded towards the spot where the speaker had appeared to be concealed the second time they had been addressed by him.

Nothing was to be seen; nothing was to be heard. They moved on towards the place from whence the voice had proceeded the first time of their hearing it. Equally unsuccessful was their pursuit.

After a considerable time thus spent in fruitless researches after the mysterious speaker by whom they had been addressed, they returned to their horses. "Nobody is to be found," said Montreville, addressing Henri.

"I feared as much, Monsieur," returned the valet.

"Feared!" echoed Montreville.

"Yes, Monsieur: I cannot help thinking that the voice resembled one that was heard the night before an old lady I once lived with in Alsace died," was the reply.

Franval had already said that the voice had appeared to him to be more than human. Henri's opinion strengthened his; and the light of the lanthorn was just sufficient to shew each that his companions' minds were occupied with unpleasant and undefined sensations.

The temper of Franval was steady, firm, and cool; and although transactions of an unexplained nature had lately occurred in his family, such as might also prepare him for a voice of warning or instruction, he did not choose to let it appear to his friend and servant, that he was moved by the occurrence just past; and therefore, with as much composure as he was able to command, he mounted his saddle, and said "As we appear to have no immediate cause to apprehend the approach of banditti, let us ride on; let us return to the road, and pursue our way."

Montreville was a young man not deficient in courage, but his disposition was tinctured with a dislike to forming acquaintance with any of the members of the world of spirits. Henri resembled him in this particular; and therefore they joyfully followed Franval's proposition of quitting the spot, where they firmly believed one of the members of the aerial community to have been flitting around them.

They continued to ride on for a considerable time without interruption; their conversation consisting merely of occasional remarks on the extraordinary adventure which they had encountered that night. When they had proceeded about a league and a half, Montreville said, "My horse knocks up; he can't go much farther without rest, I am certain; indeed, I expect that our beasts and ourselves will all be material sufferers by our want of repose, and shelter from the night air. If we could discover any habitations I should be tempted to knock at the door, in spite of what the master of the post-house said."

This observation had not been long made on the part of Montreville, ere a vivid flash of lightning passed before their eyes.

"I have foreseen a tempest some time," said Henri, "and a heavy one I think it will be; only look at the awful blackness of the clouds over our heads, Messieurs."

Franval and his friend raised their faces to the sky and felt upon them a few partial drops of rain, which announced a shower at hand. Again the lightning flashed its resplendent brilliancy upon the earth, and the thunder rolled in solemn grandeur through the sky; with each flash the tempest appeared to gather strength; with each succeeding moment the rain fell in greater quantities: and the situation of our travellers became of the most pitiable kind.

"Can we espy no cavity in the earth, no rocky dell, no place of any kind which may afford us a temporary shelter?" said Montreville; "not only the clothes we have on, but those in our saddle-bags likewise must be drenched with this heavy rain."

The mingled hail and rain, driven along by the current of a powerful north-east wind, met them full in the face; and the horses of our travellers kept continually turning to the right and to the left, in order to avoid it. At the moment Franval's horse was making a movement of this nature, a sudden flash of lightning enabled his master to descry what he could merely distinguish to be part of a wall. He communicated the observation he had made to his friend, and they immediately turned their horses towards it, in the hope of its forming part of a building which might afford them the enviable blessing of shelter from the inclemency of the weather.

As they moved on, they observed many fragments of stone scatted upon the ground, which appeared to be the ruins of a building that had either fallen into natural decay, or been crumbled by the hand of violence; and when they gained the wall which had been described by Franval, their conjectures were confirmed, for they found that it formed a part of the ruin of an ancient monastic building.

A considerable part of the front of the edifice was still standing; but, on looking through the archway in which the gate of the entrance had once been swung, the observations which they were enable to make by the momentary illumination of the passing lightning presented them only with a long perspective of gloomy ruins.

It appeared, however, probable that these ruins might afford some nook to protect them from the weather; and in this hope they dismounted; and leading their horses through the gateway, they tied them by their bridles to the remains of a massive pillar, by the side of which the wall was sufficiently high to protect them, in some measure, from the driving blast; and by the help of the lanthorn, they then proceeded to seek out for some spot which was supplied with a covering for their own heads.

A high and narrow door-way attracted them towards it: they passed through it, and found themselves within a passage partially sheltered by a roof. On one side appeared three steps of a dark marble; these they ascended, and entered an apartment which had in all probability, been the chamber of the superior at the time that the mansion had been in a state of habitation; its walls were now bare; the floor of a black oak, and in many parts broken through; and the hearth filled with fragments of stone, which had fallen upon it from the chimney.

From this apartment a single step led into a small closet, formed in the shape of an alcove, of which the floor corresponded with the former; but the walls were intersected by niches and slender pillars of stone, surmounted with compartments in fret-work, which now exhibited a striking picture of former elegance sinking under the ravaging hand of decay.

The thunder still rolled in hoarse and awful peals; and the refulgence of the forked lightning blazed at intervals through a narrow arch in the wall, which had once been the frame of a gothic and spiral window, and of which no remnants, but the iron bars, which had intersected the glass, were now remaining.

At length, after full an hour had passed in tedious expectation, the lightning became scarcely visible, and the thunder receded in gentle murmurs to the distant mountains. "Shall we return to our horses, and proceed?" said Franval.

"It still rains violently," replied Montreville; "and the darkness appears almost impenetrable."

"It is quite so, Monsieurs," said Henri. "If I might take the liberty of advising, I think it would be infinitely better, now we have a roof over our heads, to keep under it till day begins to dawn."

"But this is a sad, uncomfortable place," resumed Franval; "and if we could reconcile ourselves to enduring it in preference to being exposed to the pelting of the merciless elements, our horses must remain suffering in the wet and cold."

"They will not be the worse for that, Monsieur," returned Henri; "they are used to all weathers when they are out at pasture; and I left them bridle-room enough to enable them to pick up the grass as they stand."

"Upon my life," cried Montreville, "I am very much of Henri's opinion about remaining here till dawn of day. We are now become tolerably dry again; and should we issue out from this retreat, we shall be certain of getting wet through once more; and perhaps, after all, may not be lucky enough to find a house to refresh ourselves at. I think it would be very possible to get a comfortable nap here, wrapped up in our cloaks."

After a good deal of debate upon the subject, it was agreed that any shelter was preferable to encountering the heavy rain which continued to fall; and Montreville having wound his horseman's cloak tightly around him, lay down in one corner of the apartment with the intention beguiling an hour or two in sleep, and advised his companions to do the same.

"Had you not better, Monsieur, endeavour to compose yourself to sleep?" said Henri to his master; "this place seems to be perfectly quiet, and free from danger; and a little repose will render you the better able to bear the fatigue of travelling tomorrow."

"No," replied Franval; "I don't feel inclined to sleep; but lie you down, and take a nap, if you please." Henri availed himself of his master's permission, and stretched himself out by the side of Montreville, placing the lanthorn at his head.

Franval continued for some time to wander about the apartment where his friend and servant lay locked in the arms of sleep, till the wind, beginning to blow from another quarter to what it had before done, pierced through the stone arch of the window with chilly gusts, that induced him to seek a more sheltered situation in the adjoining closet.

In spite of those anxieties of mind which rendered him less impressive to the attacks of sleep than his companions, Franval began to feel rather weary; and seating himself upon the floor, he rested his head in niche between two of the pillars of the stone-work.

The minute he desisted from bodily exercise, the influence of sleep began to steal over his senses, and ideas to fade away under its advances. Suddenly a momentary crash made him start, and this was followed by a rumbling noise, which he had no hesitation in supposing to be caused by some mouldering fragments of the building, which had been precipitated upon the ruins below by the violence of the wind; and he again leant back his head, and closed his eyes.

Again his thoughts were wandering from the world into that confusion of ideas which accompanied the approach of sleep to a mind ill at ease within itself, when he was startled by the sound of a lengthened sigh. He sprang upon his feet; but instantly recollecting how near to him were Montreville, and his servant, he made no doubt that the sound he had heard, had been an exclamation uttered by one of them in his sleep.

He approached the door of the room where they lay, and, by the light of the lanthorn, he perceived them both still extended on the floor; and as he stood observing them, he heard Henri exclaim, "Oh, Marie! Marie!" which he knew to be the name of a little peasant girl in Brittany, who had won his heart and not doubting that the sigh he had hears, had been one which Henri had addressed to her image, which had appeared to him in his dreams, he returned to his resting place, and a third time composed himself to sleep.

He sunk to repose; but how long he had slept he was uncertain, when he was awakened by a noise resembling a gust of wind rushing through a narrow aperture; he hastily opened his eyes, and beheld object, at the sight of which the blood ran cold and trembling through his veins--He beheld the very countenance of savage expression, which he had seen through the window of the post-house; its eyes were fixed upon him, and assisted in their observation by a lighted firebrand, which the terrific form held in one of its hands. The figure of the unknown was tall and lank: the long black cloak in which it was enveloped was insufficient to hide the sharp angles of its bony stature; a hat of dark brown fur pulled down below its ears, gave a very finish of horror to its savage aspect; thus the horrible being appeared, bending forward as it stood, to gain a better view of Franval's person.

Franval started, but had not power to rise, or to speak. Instantly upon this motion on his part, with one rapid stride, the figure vanished from his sight. Its disappearance was followed by a loud clap, resembling the echo which runs through a hollow passage, after a door at its extremity has been hastily closed.

Franval attempted to call to his friend and Henri, but his tongue clove to his mouth, and refused its office. He staggered to the door of the apartment where he had left them asleep; the light which had been burning by their side, was now extinguished, or the lanthorn gone. A few minutes recovered to him the power of speech, and he called upon them both by name. Henri immediately replied to his call;

and very soon after, Montreville enquired "what was the matter?"

Through an arched window, Franval had a view of the Heavens; and he perceived that the light of day was already beginning to streak the sky. "Be not alarmed," he replied, in answer to their enquiries; "follow me into the air; I stand in need of its refreshment; and I will then explain to you what agitates me."

He darted out of the apartments and they followed him as quickly as the darkness of the place would permit; for their lamp had died in the socket, and the light of day was still so feeble, as to render objects scarcely discernible.

They found him leaning against a broken pillar, which stood in an open space apart from the mass of ruins. They approached him, renewed their enquiries; and he satisfied them with an account of what he had witnessed.

Montreville heard him with patience, but persisted in endeavouring to persuade him that the whole had been a dream, caused by the impression which had been made on his mind by the strangeness of the voice that had addressed them when amongst the trees, and the ghastly countenance which he had seen peeping through a window of the post-house. But Franval replied, "that he was certain that the figure which he had seen standing over him with a firebrand in its hand, and which he knew to be the same that he had beheld with a sensation approaching to horror when looking through the window of the post-house, had been a reality.

"Well," returned Montreville, "it is possible that this ruin may be the haunt of a banditti, of which he is one."

"I do not believe him to be a robber," replied Franval.

"Why not? What has changed your opinion of him?" asked his friend.

"I cannot say why," answered Franval; "and yet I feel my sentiments utterly changed with regard to him."

"Your ideas are bewildered by the events of the night," said Montreville.

"And then that strange voice commanding us to go to the Castle of Virandola," said Henri; "it rings in my ears yet."

"Strange indeed!" breathed forth Franval in solemn accents; and he added, "Can it be connected with him whom we seek?"

"Whithersoever we go," rejoined Montreville, "I think we had better be jogging from hence; this is not a place favourable to the combating of gloomy reflections, whether they proceed from imagination, or fact."

"No," resumed Franval; "I can't, I will not quit this spot, till I have made some investigation of the closet where I slept: I must examine whether there is a door in that particular part of the wall, at which the strange figure, whose countenance rests so forcibly on my memory, could have departed from the place: if I find any outlet, my ideas of its mortality will be confirmed."

"And if you do not?" said Montreville

"I shall still be very much tempted to believe that there is some mode of egress from the place which is not discernible to me, though known to that person, whoever he may be," answered the Chevalier.

Franval could not be argued out of his resolution of examining the closet in which he had passed the night, as soon as the light of the day should be sufficiently powerful to assist him in his investigation. Indeed, Montreville had promised to accompany Franval on his present journey from motives of pure friendship, and therefore was easily won to desist from any opposition to such plans as his friend conceived to be for his happiness.

A drizzling rain was still falling to the earth; and although the wind had much abated in strength, it still blew cold and cheerless through the long avenues of ruins; and as Franval was unwilling to return to the shelter of the apartment they had just quitted, they wandered about in order to preserve themselves from the ill effects of the cold.

After some time, Henri was, in the course of their movements, separated from his master and Montreville; and scarcely had they noticed his absence, ere they heard a pistol fired at a short distance from them. Supposing Henri to be attacked, they flew to the spot where they had parted from him, and observed him standing with his arm extended into the air, and his pistol still in it.

"Was it you who fired?" asked Franval.

"Yes," replied Henri; "and I have either brought him down, or he is run away."

"Who? who?" Impatiently demanded Franval and his friend.

"A tall fellow, wrapped in a black cloak," answered Henri, "exactly corresponding with the description my master gives of the rascal who stood gazing upon him with the firebrand in his hand. The moment that you had turned the angle of the range of pillars behind us, I observed him mounted upon the high wall; and the instant I observed him, I saw him stretch his arm towards me, and was ignorant to what end, till I saw some sparks, which convinced me that he had directed at me a pistol that had missed fire. I immediately drew mine from my girdle, and fired it at him in my own defence; and he directly disappeared; but I cannot tell whether he fell by my bullet or fled from a repetition of my fire."

"We will go to the spot, and ascertain," said Franval boldly; and immediately began to climb a pile of the ruins which led to the wall whereon Henri had seen the form. Nothing that had motion, was visible to any one of the party, when they had reached the height, which had once been a terrace projecting from the second range of windows on the side of the monastery. Many delusive shapes were to be seen, which, on close investigation, proved to be only broken arches, and decapitated pillars, which, beheld at a short

126

distance in the twilight of the morning, appeared in certain directions to assume the form of men.

They did not relax in their search, because many disappointments attended it; but it proved wholly unsuccessful; no human being was to be discerned in any part of the ruins; nor did it appear probable that Henri's pistol had wounded the one he had beheld; for as the light of day rose, they found that no spots of blood stained any part of the stone-work upon which he had appeared.

They again descended to the lower range of dilapidated grandeur, which presented itself in the romantic fragments of the mouldering abbey; and judging it now to be sufficiently light for the examination of the closet upon which Franval had resolved, they returned to that part of the building where they had passed the hours of sleep.

Montreville was the first who entered the chamber leading to the closet, and directly on stepping into it, he exclaimed, "Why, what have we here?--See--behold--characters traced upon the floor!"

Franval darted hastily forward, and beheld upon the black oak floor, these words, "Quit this place." Wrapt in astonishment and thought, he stood with his eyes fixed on the letters.

"Surely, Monsieur," cried Henri, half trembling, "it can only be a devil who plays these pranks with us."

"It is a friendly devil, however," returned Montreville, "for he warns us to get our of the way of danger; if there is any in staying here."

"I will not quit this place," cried Franval sternly, after a pause of reflective silence. "This command is to my senses, a sufficient conviction that there is some mystery to be developed by staying; and I feel impelled by a stronger sentiment than curiosity, to exert myself in order to make that discovery."

Franval rubbed one of the letters on the floor with his finger, and found that they were only written in chalk, and could easily be effaced.

"Come, pray, let us depart," said Montreville, after another pause.

"Not, at all events, till I have examined the walls of the closet," said Franval, and moved forward to the investigation. His companions followed him, and assisted in the scrutiny; but it produced only disappointment; there were an infinite number of cracks in the stone-work of the walls, but none of sufficient regularity, or length, to flatter them with the idea that it could form any part of a door, or an opening of any kind.

"I would wager my life," said Franval, "that these words were written by that horrible figure which I twice beheld in the course of last night. Surely this ruin cannot be the Castle of Virandola, of which the host spoke."

"I should imagine not," replied Montreville: "this place does not bear the appearance of ever having been a castle; every thing about it denotes it to have been a religious building."

A silence ensued; Montreville broke it: "Franval," he said, "I am certain you cannot doubt my friendship; prove to me that you have not lost that respect for the admonitions of your friend, with which you have so frequently received them at my lips: let us for the present quit this abode of mystery; let us seek some house where our bodily necessities may be attended to; and let us also employ some time in making enquiry into the report which this ruinous fabric bears in the world; and should you then still have any cause, or merely feel any wish, to make a future investigation of its secrets, I pledge my honour, that I will return with you to it, and even risk my life in assisting you through your adventure."

For a considerable time the entreaties of Montreville, seconded by those of Henri, produced no effect upon the mind of Franval: at length, after he had received a renewal of his friend's promise to return with him at some future period, if it should be his desire to make a second visit to the place they were now in, he agreed to accompany them in quest of refreshment; and information, if any were to be gained, which could assist in throwing light upon the strange adventures which had marked the last twelve hours.

Having mounted their horses, they turned into the road, and pursued the path along which they had on the former evening been journeying: at the distance of rather more than half a league from the ruin, they descried a cottage apart from the high road, and immediately rode up to it.

Before they reached the humble dwelling, the door was opened by a peasant girl of about twelve years old, who, it appeared, had seen them through a window, and been attracted by curiosity to behold travellers of so different an order of beings to those amongst whom she was accustomed to live.

Montreville called to her, and enquired whether there was any body in the cottage besides herself, and whether they would sell them any milk and bread.

The girl replied that her mother and grandmother were both within; and directly called the former, who quickly made her appearance. Having heard our travellers wants, she readily agreed to supply them in the best manner she was able; and invited them to alight, and walk in: this Montreville and Franval did: and Henri, conducted by the girl, led the horses to a stable behind the cottage, where he found a welcome of sweet, although coarse provender, for his beasts.

Franval and his friend took seats. The woman, with the garrulity natural to her sex, and her rank in life, began to inform them of her own family affairs: her husband and her sons, she said, were gone to labour on a distant part of the mountains, and she was anticipating their return with much pleasure, because they had promised to beg some grapes of the master of the vineyard for her mother, who was particularly fond of them, and who being now far advanced in years, and totally blind, had no enjoyment left her but that of the palate, which she had the least opportunity of gratifying.

This decrepit old female sat in one corner of the cottage, with her feet rested on a large stone, in order to shorten the distance at which they would else have hung from the ground, and with her chin nearly bent upon her knees.

The peasant's wife having finished the little history of her family, began to speak of the tempestuous night which was just past; and to enquire whether our travellers had rested in any part to which the tempest had extended?

"We had, indeed, a most uncomfortable lodging," replied Montreville, and informed the good woman where they had passed the night.

"It must have been uncomfortable lodging in the ruins of Saint Luke's Abbey," said the woman.

"Extremely so, I assure you," returned Montreville; "but on what account do you particularly mean?"

"The want of accommodation for sleep," she answered; "I should imagine there is scarcely a nook about it furnished with a roof."

"Yes, there is," replied Montreville, and gave a short account of the apartment they had found, with this necessary appendage for comfort against the peltings of a storm.

"But is there no other account on which you consider that it might be an unpleasant resting place?" enquired Franval.

"I dare say it is full of night birds, that shriek and scream, and make it dismal enough," replied the woman.

"Is it never disturbed with those spirits which, like the birds you speak of, do no leave their retirement, except in the shades of night?"

"What, haunted, do you mean, Messieurs?" cried the woman. "O no, blessed be the Virgin, I never heard that of the Abbey of Saint Luke. I am sure, I hardly durst live here, if such were the case;" and she crossed herself as she spoke. "No, no; one house possessed by the Devil is enough for any district."

"And have you a house of that description in your district?" asked Franval.

"You must be a stranger in these parts to ask that question, I am certain," she returned. "The Castle of Virandola, about half a league from this house, is, as I may say, a very receptacle for Satan's legions."

Franval drew his chair nearer to the woman's, and enquired of her who was its possessor.

She replied, that his name was Don Bazilio; that he and his castle were the terror of the neighbourhood; that not an individual durst approach within a considerable distance of it after dark; and that Don Bazilio was by some supposed to be a Frenchman, by some a Spaniard, and by others a Moor. Farther information on the subject she was unable to give him.

A comfortable meal was now set before them. Franval scarcely tasted it; and the perturbation of his mind appeared to increase with every minute; at length, drawing aside his friend Montreville, he told him, that he could not divest himself of the idea of the voice which had warned them to proceed to the castle of Virandola, having some connexion with the fate of Don Manuel; and that he could not satisfy himself without approaching the edifice, over which hung the impenetrable veil of mystery with which they had on the preceding evening become acquainted.

Montreville had promised to second every endeavour of his friend towards the development of Don Manuel's fate, and accordingly agreed to accompany him. As the castle was but a short distance from the cottage, they resolved to walk towards it. Franval had not yet determined to ask admittance; his present design was confined to inspecting the outside of the building, and proving whether he should

131

receive any intimation of his being expected at it by the person whose voice had admonished him to approach it. The friends informed Henri of their design, and bade him prepare to accompany them; and Franval pretending to the cottagers, that curiosity impelled him and his companions to take a view of the outside of the castle of the mysterious Don Bazilio, they asked Ricardo's grand-daughter to conduct them into the road to it. She readily complied with their request; and as they proceeded, they learnt from her replies to the questions which they had advanced to her, that there was no idea existing of Don Bazilio being himself a robber, or his castle the haunt of banditti; but that he had the repute for dealing in the black art, and that midnight was the preferred hour of his orgies, at which period strange lights had been seen flitting about the castle, and dreadful noises heard within it, by those few who at that solemn hour had ventured to approach it; but that no one, of whom she had heard, had ever attempted to gain admittance.

When the towers of the castle, rising above a rocky eminence of the rugged mountains, rendered a guide no longer necessary to the travellers, the girl ran back to her cottage; and Franval and his companions pursued their way. As they advanced towards the castle, they perceived that it had once been strongly fortified, but that its bulwarks were now fallen to decay: it presented to their view a huge pile of ancient stonework, black with age, and partially mouldering under the destructive hand of Time: gloom and awfulness were its characteristic features, and not any sign of its containing inhabitants was to be discovered about it: the drawbridge appeared no longer capable of being raised; and the moat was nearly choked up.

Our friends walked several times round its gloomy walls, and were on the point of quitting the spot, when a key, thrown from some considerable eminence, fell at the feet of the Chevalier Franval. He picked it hastily up, for he perceived that there was fastened to it a paper, on which he could distinguish the marks of hand-writing: with the most tremulous agitation he read the following words; "This key opens the door in the western turret; enter it at the return of night." If these words excited the astonishment of the Chevalier Franval, what was the emotion with which he beheld the paper signed by the name of Rodalvo, the faithful and respected servant of Don Manuel!

The paper fastened to the key, by directing them to return at night, appeared to warn them to retire for the present from the site of the castle, which they accordingly did.

The emotion of Franval's soul was so great at the belief that he had discovered the retreat of his beloved sister's husband, that he was incapable of expressing his feelings. Equally tongue-tied by astonishment were his friend Montreville, and his servant Henri. They returned to the cottage, and seated themselves on a bench by the door, where some degree of composure gradually returning to their minds, they at length began to give expression to their ideas: but to form conjectures was all they were still able to do; it was impossible for them to decide by what power Don Manuel was detained an inmate of the Mysterious Castle of Virandola, as his servant's being an inhabitant of it seemed to bespeak that he was; or to ascertain what connexion there could be between him and the universally dreaded Don Bazilio.

They now doubted not that the voice which had on the preceding evening admonished them to proceed to the Castle of Virandola, had been that of Rodalvo; but they were at a loss whether or not to suppose that the terrific being who had twice been seen by Franval, and once by his servant Henri, was the owner of the castle.

The agitation of mind in which the day was passed by them all, especially by the Chevalier Franval, may be easily conjectured. They were entertained with hospitality and kindness at the cottage, but the attentions of their hostess and her family were often unheeded by them; and the natural impatience of their minds, rendered the day, in appearance, the longest they had ever known.

THE MYSTERIOUS SPANIARD

When the shades of night had fallen to the earth, Franval and his companions set out on their mysterious expedition. The night was cloudy, scarcely a star gemmed the face of Heaven; the crescent of an infant moon rising above the distant mountains, threw a faint and silvery light upon partial spots of the landscape. Having reached the castle, they sought out the western turret, of which the situation could not be mistaken; and Franval applied the key to the lock: with little difficulty the door was opened by him, and they all three entered. Total darkness prevailed within, and they stood debating, how to proceed. Suddenly a distant light gleamed upon the scene, and they perceived that it was reflected through a spiral window of stained glass, at the extremity of a spacious hall in which they were standing. The light was no sooner beheld, than it again vanished: it had, however, been sufficient to shew our adventurers that they might proceed for a considerable space without the danger of falling, as the momentary illumination had been sufficient for them to perceive that there were no intervening steps between the door which they had entered and the opposite wall. Franval drew his sword; and extending before him the arm which bore it, as a protection to his person, he moved cautiously on. He continued his progress for some time, till a flaming firebrand, carried in the hand of some being whose pace was so swift as not to give him time to behold its person, darted across his path; and he observed, by the temporary influence of the light, that he had wandered into a lofty and narrow passage.

He stopped a moment, and listened; no sound met his ear; and he concluded, from the silence, that he had strayed from his companions. He, however, resolved not to suffer his courage to forsake him, or to relax in his attempt at developing the mystery of the place, to which act he had been summoned by one connected with a man whom he did not esteem less on his own account, than as the nearest relative of his beloved sister: using, therefore, every precaution which his perilous situation permitted him to do for guarding against accident, he still proceeded.

Suddenly a deep groan struck his ear; it was followed by a stifled shriek; and these sounds were succeeded by several voices, uttering such tones as might have been expected from demons uttering expressions of delight. Again all was still; and the next moment the Chevalier, moving a step or two from the spot where he had been standing, found himself upon so rapid a declivity, as obliged him to move on, whether it met his inclination or not.

This declivity continued, as nearly as Franval could conjecture, for at least the space of an hundred feet; and whilst descending it, he heard a repetition of the dreadful sounds to which he had before listened.

At length he felt himself again upon even ground; there was now no longer any pavement under his feet, but a loose and crumbling earth. Here he paused an instant: he wished for the society of his friend and Henri, but the wish was in vain: it was now evident that the darkness of the place had separated them from each other. An infinite satisfaction would it have been to his feelings, had Rodalvo now appeared to him, and either directed his progress, or given him some explanation of the existing mystery. Whilst he stood debating thus with his own mind, he heard the voice of some one either in solemn prayer, or reading emphatically aloud; which of the two he could not distinguish; and turning his eyes around on every side, a faint light, playing on a distant wall, met his sight; he moved towards it, and pursuing the direction in which it shone, ascended a few steps, cut, as it seemed, out of the rugged earth, which led him to an eminence, from whence he looked down upon a scene which almost froze his blood in its current to his heart.

Some few feet below the surface of the spot on which he stood, was what appeared to him a spacious cavern; it was illuminated by several firebrands, which were stuck into the earth at certain distances from each other, and of which the pitchy tops sent forth darting flames, which climbed like fiery serpents towards the dusky roof. At the extremity of the place, in letters which appeared the colour of transparent blood, was deciphered the word "VENGEANCE;" and

135

immediately under this inscription, in a chair, on the back of which were fixed three human skulls, and on either side of which stood a ghastly skeleton, sat the very being whom Franval had on the preceding evening beheld, first through the window of the post-house, and next bending over him with a lighted firebrand in his hand, amidst the ruins of Saint Luke's Abbey; the being whom, from the account which he had heard of the possessor of the castle, he could not doubt to be Don Bazilio himself nor were his suspicions incorrect.

On either side of him, seated around a table of a semi-circular form, were several other persons, habited like himself, in loose garments, with hats of dark fur, of which the brims were drawn down around their faces, and added to the terrific appearance of their countenances, already sufficiently dreadful to the view.

Before the table, and immediately opposite to Don Bazilio, knelt a human figure, nearly naked, and whose limbs were shaking with a violent trembling, produced either by cold or apprehension; and judging, from his own feelings, at the scene before him, Franval could not doubt it to be the latter. Around him were placed six familiars, in the habits of demons, each directing at him an instrument of death, which they were prepared to thrust to his heart, if a signal were given them to that effect.

A few moments observation clearly proved to Franval, that the kneeling man was a recipient, about to be admitted a member of some secret community, the lawless transactions of which he was to be terrified from divulging. The solemn voice which he had heard on his approach to the spot of terror which he was now contemplating, he found to have been that of Don Bazilio, who was still reading from a volume, extended before him on the table, the obligations to which the novice, at that moment initiating into the mysteries of the community, was called upon to swear observance.

The first of these obligations to which Franval heard Don Bazilio call upon the recipient to subscribe, contained these words: "Swear to divulge no secret with which you are made acquainted by the community, to any being unconnected with it; and to report every one with which you may be entrusted by other persons to it."

"I swear," replied the recipient: and the expression of satisfaction with which the assembly received his acquiescence, explained to Franval what had been the shouts of joy that had before heard when at a distance from the cavern.

Again Don Bazilio read; "If thou refuse to comply with any command issued to thee by the authority before whom thou kneelest, recollect that the sword of their revenge will fall on thee quicker than the lightning; remember this; and swear that, in assisting the vengeance they are leagued to perpetrate, neither the life of thy father, mother, wife, nor child, of thy dearest friend, or nearest connection, shall be regarded by thee."

The recipient did not immediately reply. "Swear instantly," cried Don Bazilio, "or I pronounce the signal that shall seal thy death." He raised himself upon his seat as he spoke. Franval believed the last moment of the kneeling man to be at hand, and the exclamation of "Oh, merciful God!" burst from his lips.

His voice was heard by the members of the assembly; and turning their eyes to the spot from whence it had proceeded, they no sooner beheld him, than several of them sprang from their seats, and flying up to an ascent which led to the eminence where Franval stood, they seized his person, and dragged him down into the centre of the cavern.

"Who art thou?" exclaimed Don Bazilio, "who hast dared intrude upon our privacy? and by what means hast thou gained access to this spot?" Whilst speaking, he advanced towards Franval; and when he had approached sufficiently near to him to distinguish his features, he added, "Ha! I have beheld thee before in a situation to which I cannot doubt thou camest as a spy upon my actions. The ruined Abbey of St. Luke is the spot to which I refer. Under the impression which thy conduct has raised in my mind, thou can'st not live." Then turning to the familiars around him, he cried, "Bring the cord, and do your duty."

No sooner had Don Bazilio issued this command, than the recipient, moving forward, threw himself on his knees before him, and, in a voice of the humblest supplication, he exclaimed, "Oh spare him! I entreat, I implore you, for my sake spare him; he is the brother of my beloved wife!"

The tones in which the kneeling man spoke, were familiar to the ear of Franval; he turned his eyes upon him, and, to his utter astonishment, beheld in him Don Manuel di Vadilla!

After a few instants of private conversation with another member of the occult community, Don Bazilio commanded Franval to be led to the grated cell. The familiars immediately seized his arms, and, preceded by one of their fellows, who lighted them with a torch which he had torn up from its station in the floor of the cavern, they forced him along several winding passages, which ultimately brought them to the grated dungeon, into which they thrust him, and then departed, taking away with them the light.

The torturing and perplexing sensations which at this period filled the breast of the Chevalier Franval, may be easily imagined. What could he suppose would be the event of his present situation? what could be the mystery which bound together the community before whose authority he had beheld the unfortunate Don Manuel, kneeling an apparent victim? Where now, he wondered, were his friends Montreville and Henri: had they, like himself, fallen into the power of the mystic band by whom the castle was habited, had they escaped their toils?

About the midnight hour, through the grating of his prison, he beheld a light approaching: in a few minutes it drew sufficiently near to him for him to distinguish that it was borne in the hand of Don Bazilio; he placed himself opposite to the grated window of Franval's cell, and thus addressed him: "Stranger, having beheld as much as you have done of the mysteries of this place, there is but one point left for you to decide upon; you must either forfeit your life to our safety, or bind yourself by the vows which connect our community."

"Your terms," replied Franval, "appear as extraordinary as your mysteries; you must inform me what the latter are, and to what purpose they are maintained, ere I can consent, or refuse, to subscribe to them."

"I intend to do so," returned Don Bazilio. "I fear not to entrust to you the secret, because within the next twenty hours, you must, as I have already declared to you, become one of us, or cease to exist. Had it not been for the intercession of the young man who is known to you by the name of Don Manuel, you had not at this moment been alive to receive my offer. Now then attend: I am not a Spaniard, as my name implies me to be; I am by birth a Frenchman. My elder brother was the Marquis de la Croix; myself the Chevalier of the same name. It is now about eighteen years since by brother, and another gentleman, were alike suppliants to the crown for the permission of acceding to a Duchy which at that moment lay dormant; and, in the line of succession to which, they both stood with apparently equal rights; it rested consequently on the breast of the monarch on whom the honour should be conferred; and, after having deceived my brother with false hopes, the King bestowed the contested title on his competitor. Was not this a disappointment sufficiently strong to drive almost to madness a man of proud spirit? for such was my brother; and whose pride was supported by a consciousness of having devoted not only his active services, but his purse, to his King and his country. He immediately quitted the course, vowing never to return to it again.

"My brother was, at the period of which I am speaking, a widower; from his wife, who had been a Spanish lady of considerable distinction, he had inherited this castle of

Virandola; and hither he retired, accompanied by myself, and three other friends, peculiarly attached to his interests.

"We had not been here many days ere he thus addressed us. 'My friends, I am sufficiently well acquainted with your attachment to me, to be conscious that I may disclose to you the inmost sentiments of my hear in full assurance of your secrecy. Listen, then to my words: as we have not in our power any present means of revenging the failure of my just and high-raised expectation, let us have the glory of founding a sect, which shall grow by our rearing, privately and unsuspectedly, from the small number here collected, into a magnitude which shall eventually crush the exercise of such unlimited power as I have been a sufferer from."

"We applauded his idea, and entered with fervour into his plan: we immediately bound ourselves by the most solemn oath which could pass the lips of man, to act by every exertion of our ability towards the subversion of every earthly power, by the possession of which one man is raised to a superiority over his fellows: we swore that not even the peace or safety of our dearest connections should obstruct us in the progress of our design; and moreover, that we would use every means of adding members to our secret community."

"From that instant we became a sect of Illuminati; we frequented lodges of masonry, and all public societies; we probed the hearts of their members, and when we found individuals suited to our purpose, we conducted them hither; and in the cavern which you have this night beheld, we initiated them into our mysteries.

"At the expiration of twelve years, my brother died; he fell the victim of a disorder which was slow in its progress; and as he was conscious of the approach of death, he appointed me the guardian of his only child, who was a son named Lewis, at that time in his fifteenth year; and concerning the future conduct of whose life he gave me the most particular and impressive directions.

"For many reasons, my brother and myself had for some time assumed the name of Vadilla, and professed ourselves to be Spaniards; and that of Lewis had, for the sake of accordance with our own, been changed to Manuel. Thus you perceive that the husband of your sister is my nephew."

Franval did not reply, and Don Bazilio continued thus:

"My deceased brother had enjoined me to initiate his son into the mysteries of our society when he had attained the age of twenty-one years, and to inform him that it had been the dying request of his father, that he would never form any connections in life, above all, that of marriage; but devote himself entirely to the forwarding of those views which had been planned by his parent; and which that parent conceived he might be less strenuous in pursuing, if he were bound by any other ties, which might claim at least an equal share of his feelings.

"At the age of eighteen, I informed him of his father's wish that he should lead a life of celibacy; and informed him that, at the age of twenty-one, a secret of the utmost importance would be entrusted to him, and business of the most interesting and peculiar nature placed in his hands; for devoting himself entirely to the services of which, I wished him, in the intermediate time, to prepare his mind, as it had been the dying request of his father that he should do so. He was become accustomed, by habit, to behold an air of mystery pervading the countenances of such inhabitants of the castle as were in my confidence, and had been in that of his deceased father; and my words did not appear so much to surprise him, as I had expected they would. He had hitherto not been the distance of more than four or five leagues from the Castle of Virandola, and he petitioned me to suffer him to travel for two or three years: to this request I consented, on condition of his promising to return to me against the period of his completing his twenty-first year, and of his forming no connection, or engagement, in the world, upon which he was about to enter. He gave me his promise to this effect. I furnished him with a most liberal supply of money, which I was with the greatest ease enabled to do, from the wealth of

141

my deceased brother; and placing him under the care of a man named Rodalvo, the only domestic in my brother's service who had been admitted into our secret community, I permitted him to depart.

"By mutual agreement, I was not to receive any letter from my nephew during his absence. At length arrived his twenty-first birthday, and he was not returned. Several months passed on, and still he came not. I felt dissatisfied at the apparently ungrateful use which he had made of my indulgence; and I employed spies to discover for me where he loitered. Judge my disappointment and anger, when I learnt, in the course of time, from these persons, that he had broken through every injunction which I had given him, and was become a husband and a father. Against Rodalvo, also, was my rage excited, for not having withheld him from forming ties so opposite to the will of his late father.

"Having gained the knowledge of his retreat, I commissioned some of the inferior members of our occult society to lie in ambush for him and Rodalvo, to seize their persons, and to reconduct them to this castle. On their way to your villa, my emissaries were so fortunate as to meet them in Paris; where, having hurried them into a closed carriage, they set off with them, without delay, for the frontiers of the kingdom.

"Several accidents, which they met with on the road, so materially delayed their progress, that they did not till the afternoon of yesterday, reach the post-house before which you and your companions stopped last night.

"Impatience to behold my nephew, and reason with him on his disobedience to my injunctions, had brought me to the post-house to meet him; and as I found that he could not be prevailed upon, although in my power, by gentle means, to proceed to the Castle of Virandola, I resolved not to conduct him to it till the dead hour of midnight, when we should not be liable to encounter any observers of his conduct; and having resolved to remain till that hour at the post-house, I bound the host by a handsome bribe, and an oath, not to admit any one into it whilst we continued his inmates: how faithfully he performed his trust, you are already acquainted.

"Whilst we remained in the post-house, I questioned my nephew on the reason which had induced him to act in opposition to the conduct I had marked out for him to follow; and he confessed to me, that he had, by his supplications and entreaties, won Rodalvo into confessing to him, the cause for which he had been so earnestly enjoined to return, at the age of twenty-one, to the Castle of Virandola; and that abhorring, as he expressed himself, the nature and object of our community, immediately on having gained this knowledge, he determined never to accede to the plan which had been proposed for his future life, but to strike out one which he himself deemed more capable of producing his happiness. Having done this, he procured Rodalvo's promise never to quit his service; and in the course of time, he became the husband of your sister. Sufficient honour, however, was still left to him to resolve never to betray the secret of our community, out of respect to the safety of me, his uncle.

"In the Ruins of Saint Luke's Abbey, where you last night found shelter from the storm, is the entrance to a subterranean passage which leads into vaults beneath the Castle of Virandola; and this passage is in constant use by the members of our secret community, in order to protect them from being seen, and recognised, in entering or quitting the castle, as might chance to occur were they always to pass through its gates. By this passage I had last night resolved to reconduct my nephew; and having seen him safely guarded through it's entrance, I was about to follow him, when, hearing the sound of a voice amidst the ruins, I judged it not impossible that it might proceed from some brother of our society, who might have lost his way in the darkness amongst them. Lighted by the firebrand which I carried in my hand, I proceeded towards the spot from whence the sound had proceeded, and discovered you and your companions stretched on the ground asleep. The moment I beheld you, I believed you to be one of the travellers whom I had before seen refused admittance into the post-house: and as I bent over you, to ascertain if my conjecture were just, you awoke, and turned upon me your eyes. To avoid, as much as possible, your observation, I darted precipitately through a concealed door in the wall, which led to a branch in the subterranean passage of which I have already spoken to you.

"When I had quitted your sight, I began to doubt whether you and your companions were really weary travellers, or spies upon me, or the place ye were in, and counterfeiting sleep, the better to cover you purpose: I accordingly determined to watch your actions. From the spot of my concealment, I heard your footsteps quitting the dilapidated chamber, and I followed you amidst the ruin. Your servant beheld me turn an angle of the walls: I levelled my pistol at him, and it missed fire: my aim had not been to wound him, but to alarm you all, and send you away from the spot. I was foiled in this attempt: but still I pursued your steps unseen by you, and hearing you express a desire of returning to the apartment where you had slept, I resolved to repair thither before you and to mark the floor with the words of warning which you found upon it. 'Quit this place,' was the sentence I wrote; and seeing you shortly after mount your horses and depart, I congratulated myself on having procured the end I desired, by means which, probably, appeared to you of the greatest mystery; and having done so, I immediately proceeded to the castle.

"I thought of you no more throughout the day: it was passed by me in preparations for the admission of Don Manuel into our secret community; to be present at which ceremony, I had invited all the principal members of our society. The initiation was proceeding successfully, though I confess with evident reluctance on the part of the recipient, when the exclamation you uttered assailed our ears. I instantly recognised your person; and another minute would have sealed your fate in death, had not Don Manuel, to my utter astonishment, pleaded for mercy to be shewn to you, as the brother of his wife.

"A request made to the community by one of its members, is never refused to him without due deliberation being first given to it; and as we deemed Don Manuel to have proceeded so far in his initiation, as to be entitled to rank as one of us, his petition was heard, and you conveyed to prison.

"My immediate concern was then to examine by what means you had gained admittance into this castle; and to cause a diligent search to be made for your companions, who I supposed might also have entered it: they could not be discovered; but a paper, tied to a key found in the door of the western turret, directing you to return at night, and signed Rodalvo, explained at once how you had gained entrance, and who was the traitor that merited the vengeance of the community.

"I caused him instantly to be dragged by my familiars to my feet: the fact of his own handwriting he could not deny; his every nerve appeared to be unstrung with terror; and instead of attempting to exculpate himself, he increased my knowledge of his guilt, by confessing, that, having recognized your voice last night on the outside of the post-house, his desire of informing you where to find Don Manuel, of whom he could not doubt that you were in search, led him to steal out of the post-house, and to pursue you on a mule, which he took from one of the stables; and that, having overtaken you, he enjoined you to proceed to the Castle of Virandola; but durst not stay to converse with you, lest his absence from the post-house should have been discovered by me, and punished with death."

"Whatever my fate may be," exclaimed Franval, "let me entreat your mercy to that kind old man."

"It is too late," returned Don Bazilio; "he had twice been faithless to his trust: my poniard has drunk his blood."

"Unhappy man!" replied the Chevalier: "he will be rewarded in Heaven; for his errors were on the side of Virtue."

Don Bazilio uttered an exclamation of contempt, and, after a momentary pause, spoke thus:

"Now, to my most important business with you, Chevalier: by the interference of my nephew, your life has hitherto been miraculously preserved to you; it now rests entirely with yourself, how long you wish to retain that blessing of yours. To-morrow night you must either become a member of this community, or share the fate of Rodalvo: the intervening twenty-four hours will be give you for forming your determination."

"I require not an instant," returned Franval: "the vows which bind your infamous society can never pass my lips: truth and loyalty to my sovereign, and his adherents, glow with true fervour in my breast. Beneath the authority which sways this land, my father prospered; he conducted the battles which upheld it: and his son will sooner expire on the rack, than nourish a thought towards its destruction."

"The hour of proof will come," replied Don Bazilio. "Tomorrow night at twelve—Remember!" and he departed.

No one again appeared to disturb the silence of Franval's prison throughout the night; and the rugged earth, barely covered with a lock of straw, was his resting-place. In the morning Don Bazilio again appeared; he was followed by an attendant, who, through the gratings of Franval's prison, placed upon a shelf immediately below the opening a small loaf of coarse bread, and a cup of muddy water.

"Under the resolution by which I left you swayed last night," said Don Bazilio, "this wretched fare must be yours; if you are become a proselyte to my opinion, you may command whatever your please."

"I am not become so, nor shall I ever," returned Franval.

"Remember what is to be the issue of the approaching night," said Don Bazilio emphatically, and again retired.

In the utmost wretchedness passed the hours of the Chevalier Franval: he had no other fate to expect from the merciless beings into whose hands he had fallen, than a death of savage torture; and no consolation under his affliction, except that which he derived from the conviction that it was better to die, than to lay a load of guilt upon his conscience.

At last arrived the hour of Franval's trial; it was announced to him by the beams of torches playing on the walls of his prison, and numerous footsteps approaching towards it. Several men, dressed in similar habits to those whom he had beheld on the preceding night, led him forth, and conducted him into the cavern of horrors, where he found the blood-thirsty community over whom Don Bazilio presided, assembled: He looked anxiously around, in the hope of espying amongst the number Don Manuel, but he saw him not.

Savageness, horror, and malignancy, were portrayed on every countenance; and each appeared to grin with exultation, and a mixture of contempt, on Franval. The place was lighted by firebrands, as on the preceding night, and every regulation appeared the same. After a short pause, Don Bazilio spoke; he repeated to Franval, that his life could only be preserved to him by his accepting the vows of the society; and concluded by informing him, that three questions were about to be proposed to him, and that if his replies to them all were unsatisfactory to the community, his death would immediately ensue.

Franval still answered with the same firmness and resolution which his conscience had before dictated to him.

Warning him once more to consider well his intention ere he drew upon himself the sword of vengeance, Don Bazilio proposed to him the first question; pointing, as he spoke, to the inscription above the chair upon which he sat.

"Wilt thou," said he, "bend thy body in obedience to the attribute of our society, Vengeance?"

"I will not," Franval replied.

"Wilt thou kneel, and pray for the approach of that day which shall give equality to men?" was the second question.

"I will not," again replied Franval.

"Hadst thou rather submit to death thyself, than cause the death of one placed in a situation of power over thee?" was the substance of the third question.

"I had," replied Franval firmly.

"Take then the reward of thy stubbornness," cried Don Bazilio. "Familiars, do your duty."

Instantly Franval felt himself seized by many hands: a cloth was thrown over his head; and he expected immediately to feel the steel piercing his heart; when, at the very instant, a crash like thunder rent the castle: it was repeated a second, a third, and a fourth time, with increased violence.

"We are betrayed!" cried Don Bazilio. "Comrades, defend yourselves."

"The hands which held Franval, were now withdrawn; and, snatching the cloth from his head, he beheld the cavern entered by a band of soldiery, who, rushing upon the Illuminati, made them in a few minutes their prisoners; and the next instant Montreville and Henri were by the side of Franval."

The tide of joy which rushed into the heart of the Chevalier Franval, every breast of feeling must be capable of estimating; but it is necessary that we should give a detail of the happy cause which led to this unexpected event.

When Montreville and Henri had, on the preceding night, been separated by the darkness in the castle hall from Franval, they wandered about for a considerable time, without being able to make any progress into the building. Franval did not return to them. Strange noises met their ears: their sight was started by one of the familiars of the secret community in his demon's dress, passing before them with a lighted firebrand in his hand; and their apprehensions being raised, not only for their companion, but for themselves, they resolved to seek assistance for enquiring into the fate of him from whom they had been separated.

Thus determined, they precipitately quitted the castle, and returning to the cottage where they had been entertained throughout the day, they took their horses from the stable, and having mounted them, rode with all speed towards the nearest garrison town on the frontiers of France: they reached it early in the morning, and having laid an account of their adventure before the police in terms which excited them to an immediate investigation of the truth, they selected fifty of the soldiery, under the command of a trusty officer, to accompany Montreville without delay to the Castle of Virandola. They marched with as much expedition as a body of men bearing arms were able to do, and reached the castle about the hour of midnight: they immediately forced themselves an entrance into the building; and dispersing different ways, a considerable number of them met in the cavern of horrors, as has already been related, at the critical moment of Franval's fate.

As soon as the members of the infamous community of vengeance were secured, and Franval convinced of his safety from the mouths of his friend and servant, a search was made in the castle, in order to ascertain whether it contained any unhappy beings suffering beneath the inhumanity of the terrific horde by which it had been infested: the first object of horror which was discovered by the scrutineers, was the body of the unfortunate Rodalvo, who had fallen the victim of his affection for his master: the next was Don Manuel himself, who was chained to the walls of a flinty dungeon, where he had been fated by his relentless uncle to remain till the Chevalier Franval had either pronounced the vows which were to constitute him a member of the society, or paid the forfeit of his refusal in death.

The grief which Don Manuel had experienced at being torn from the arms of his beloved wife, and dragged to the execution of a purpose at which his soul revolted, could only be equalled by the ecstasy with which he beheld himself and Franval again at liberty, and dwelt on his return to his adored Amarylla, and his infant children.

The rage of Don Bazilio's disappointed soul expressed itself solely in sullen silence. By the command of the police in the town from whence Montreville had procured military assistance, the band of Illuminati were conveyed in chains to Paris, to take their public trial; and on their arrival there, the Chevalier Franval, Montreville, and Don Manuel, whom we must now know by his real name of the Marquis de la Croix, were detained to give evidence against them.

Before the day of trial arrived, Don Bazilio gave a most unquestionable proof of his consciousness of his past guilt, and of the present wretched state of his mind, by putting an end to his own existence in prison. By the voice of the law, his associates in iniquity were adjudged to die beneath the hand of the executioner; which sentence was put into effect on the third day after their condemnation.

On the Chevalier Franval, and the Marquis de la Croix, the King, in addition to other high marks of his favour, bestowed an immense pecuniary reward from the coffers of the state. And the united voice of a rejoicing people bestowed on them the tribute of public applause, for having been the instruments through which retribution and punishment had been inflicted on a set of beings, sufficiently depraved and worthless, to have been brooding the subversion of a prosperous state, and the fall of a virtuous monarch.

Happy in the consciousness of having acted as it became virtuous and loyal subjects to have done, and grateful to Providence for its invisible interposition in the fate of the excellent young Marquis, they returned to the Chevalier's villa crowned with triumph and delight, where the caresses they received from an affectionate sister, and adored wife, rendered them the most enviable men whom the kingdom of France could boast. The society of vengeance being scattered to the winds, the Chevalier and his brother instituted a community of Benevolence to celebrate its destruction. Great was the honour of being admitted a member, and unsullied the virtuous principles of those who became so.

The children of de la Croix, as they grew to manhood, considered it their glory to be descended from those who had sown the seeds of so praiseworthy a society; and their lovely mother, stretching over them in affection and joy, appeared the earthly representative of that goddess of Benevolence, to whom a temple was raised in all their hearts.

Another book you may like…

THE WORKS OF
EDGAR ALLAN POE
THE "RAVEN" EDITION
VOLUME 1

Benediction Classics, 2011
Hardcover, 236 pages
ISBN-10: 1849025517, ISBN-13: 978-1-84902-551-5
Volume One of a new five-volume edition of Poe's works, based on the Raven edition of 1903. It includes three articles about Edgar Allan Poe and the tales 'The Unparalleled Adventures of one Hans Pfaal', 'The Gold-Bug', 'Four Beasts in One - the Homo-Cameleopard', 'The Murders in the Rue Morgue', 'The Mystery of Marie Rogêt', 'The Balloon-Hoax', 'Ms. Found in a Bottle' and 'The Oval Portrait'.

Also from Benediction Books ...

Wandering Between Two Worlds: Essays on Faith and Art
Anita Mathias
Benediction Books, 2007
152 pages
ISBN: 0955373700

Available from www.amazon.com, www.amazon.co.uk

In these wide-ranging lyrical essays, Anita Mathias writes, in lush, lovely prose, of her naughty Catholic childhood in Jamshedpur, India; her large, eccentric family in Mangalore, a sea-coast town converted by the Portuguese in the sixteenth century; her rebellion and atheism as a teenager in her Himalayan boarding school, run by German missionary nuns, St. Mary's Convent, Nainital; and her abrupt religious conversion after which she entered Mother Teresa's convent in Calcutta as a novice. Later rich, elegant essays explore the dualities of her life as a writer, mother, and Christian in the United States-- Domesticity and Art, Writing and Prayer, and the experience of being "an alien and stranger" as an immigrant in America, sensing the need for roots.

About the Author

Anita Mathias is the author of Wandering Between Two Worlds: Essays on Faith and Art. She has a B.A. and M.A. in English from Somerville College, Oxford University, and an M.A. in Creative Writing from the Ohio State University, USA. Anita won a National Endowment of the Arts fellowship in Creative Nonfiction in 1997. She lives in Oxford, England with her husband, Roy, and her daughters, Zoe and Irene.

Visit Anita at http://www.anitamathias.com, and on http://theoxfordchristian.blogspot.com, her Christian blog; http://wanderingbetweentwoworlds.blogspot.com/, her personal blog, and http://thegoodbooksblog.blogspot.com, her literary and writing blog.

The Church That Had Too Much
Anita Mathias
Benediction Books, 2010
52 pages
ISBN: 9781849026567

Available from www.amazon.com, www.amazon.co.uk

The Church That Had Too Much was very well-intentioned. She wanted to love God, she wanted to love people, but she was both hampered by her muchness and the abundance of her possessions, and beset by ambition, power struggles and snobbery. Read about the surprising way The Church That Had Too Much began to resolve her problems in this deceptively simple and enchanting fable.

About the Author

Anita Mathias is the author of Wandering Between Two Worlds: Essays on Faith and Art. She has a B.A. and M.A. in English from Somerville College, Oxford University, and an M.A. in Creative Writing from the Ohio State University, USA. Anita won a National Endowment of the Arts fellowship in Creative Nonfiction in 1997. She lives in Oxford, England with her husband, Roy, and her daughters, Zoe and Irene.

Visit Anita at http://www.anitamathias.com, and on http://theoxfordchristian.blogspot.com, her Christian blog; http://wanderingbetweentwoworlds.blogspot.com/, her personal blog, and http://thegoodbooksblog.blogspot.com, her literary and writing blog.